LOV8 KiLLS

SID

&

nancy

ALEX COX & ABBE WOOL

When the script was originally written it was called *Love Kills*, but for bullshit legalistic reasons the film may end up being called *Sid and Nancy* – which is just too bad.

SID AND NANCY

ALEX COX & ABBE WOOL

First published in 1986 by
Faber and Faber Limited
3 Queen Square, London WC1N 3AU
Printed in Great Britain by
Redwood Burn Limited, Trowbridge, Wiltshire

© Alex Cox and Abbe Wool 1986

British Library Cataloguing in Publication Data

Cox, Alex
Sid and Nancy
I. Title
822' · 914

II. Wool, Abbe
PR6053 · 096/

ISBN 0-571-14545-0

———————   ———————

Cover photograph by Simon Mein
Stills photography by Simon Mein (UK)
Joe Stevens (USA)
Design by MX/SA at Assorted iMaGes, London
Cover design based on original designs by Jamie Reid
Typesetting by Midas Graphics

CONTENTS

———— ————

*Sid and Nancy opened in London
on July 25th 1986*

Sid Vicious — a nasty piece of work. Very nasty. I saw him in the bathroom at the Country Club, jacking up. He had this huge black bodyguard in there. The guy picked me up, turned me around and threw me out.

JEREMY

In the 1920s, when I was living in the Residencia there was a double suicide in Madrid. A student and his young fiancée killed themselves in a restaurant garden. They were known to be passionately in love; their families were on excellent terms with each other; and when an autopsy was performed, the girl was found to be a virgin . . .
    So why the double suicide? I still don't have the answer, except that perhaps a truly passionate love, a sublime love that's reached a certain peak of intensity, is simply incompatible with life itself. Perhaps it's too great, too powerful. Perhaps it can exist only in death.

LUIS BUÑUEL, My Last Sigh

ALEX:
In 1980 I tried to write a screenplay called *Too Kool To Die*. It was about an English rock 'n' roll band in America. About half-way through writing it I realized that the most interesting thing in the story wasn't the singer or the guitarist or the drummer. It was the bass player and his girl. What became of them was ten times more interesting than what happened to the band. The pair of them were this incredible unit, very bad in many ways, but more than just two isolated, paranoid, lonely individuals. They were Sid and Nancy.

It's important to relate the sentimentality; the real truth. Even if it's sentimental and kind of corny, it's all right. They were human beings. There were what society produced. They were the real specimens of rock 'n' roll.

DEBBIE

ABBE:
What makes it tragic is that they were kids. They were very street-wise kids and so you sort of think, 'Oh they're so hard'. But everyone when they're really in love is the same: you get these rushes of 'I am going to die with this

person' and it's really overwhelming. In the best part of their relationship they were caught up in that. But because of who they were, they meant it a little too much.

> *When you really love someone you stay with them no matter what the problems are. Everybody was angry then, but not at anything in particular. The worst time for their relationship was when they got bad press. Sid would get upset and Nancy would get upset as well. I couldn't see them ever splitting up. You meet some people and you click with them and you always love each other.*
>
> HEIDI

ALEX:

I came to London and I started meeting people who had known them. Wherever I went, it seemed like I'd meet someone who had gone to the launderette with Sid and Nancy, or reported them to the police, or been their friend. These people turned me on to other people. I made lots of notes. We started writing the outline in New York in late December 1984. We stayed at the Chelsea Hotel. The first night I was there somebody called me up at two a.m. saying 'Sid? Sid? Sid?' Behind the mirror on the bedroom wall was written, SID VICIOUS WAS INNOCENT, NANCY R.I.P.

> *They were in love. They were completely dependent on each other. They were also in love with smack. They were really weak characters. We'd see them nodding out at the back tables at Max's and throwing chairs at people who came in. No one kicked them out and we thought they were really cool. I was a naïve young kid and didn't know from heroin. They had cool haircuts and their parents didn't shout at them. They obviously didn't have to work real jobs because of the haircuts. They were Sid and Nancy, rock 'n' roll stars, and they had every right to be there.*
>
> NINA

ABBE

There are a lot of different theories about how did Nancy die, who really killed Nancy and all that. When we first started writing the script, we went through a long process of 'How are we going to deal with all these theories? Is this going to be a murder mystery? Or are we just going to make up something that fits dramatically?' And a lot of people said yeah, they were just so fucked up at that moment, their lives had just completely disintegrated, they were in this teeny little space. They were going to die, one way or the other . . .

ALEX:

What the actors did with the end of *Sid and Nancy* differs completely from what we scripted. I think it's only to the good because they lived closer to the characters of Sid and Nancy then Abbe and I did. By the time we shot the final scenes, Chloe was really Nancy and Gary was really Sid. Their ending is better than anything we could have written. I had this revelation sitting on the set one night, alone: that what Gary and Chloe had just shown me wasn't simply good acting — it was really true.

> *Sid showed me his collection of weapons. Sharpened studded wristbands. Knives. 'I could really mark you with this if I wanted to.' 'But you wouldn't, would you, Sid?' 'No.' The room was full of leather clothes and Nancy's underwear. The TV was on. I didn't risk the bathroom. Nancy went in there and groans started coming out. Sid said she had something wrong with her kidneys. He fetched her out and she lay down and cried and Sid stroked her head.*

> ROSALIND

ALEX:
Sid is a real character. A lot of people still revere him. He's a British institution, like the Beefeater or the Queen Mother or John Bull. Sid's like Arthur Askey or Eric Sykes or Hattie Jacques. It's about time Nancy was put in the same mythic pantheon as Sid. Sid wouldn't be shit without Nancy. He'd probably be around today, playing in some awful band.

ABBE:
I had a dream that Nancy came to visit me and she told me she was really happy we were making the film because it was going to set her mother's story straight. I feel a near-psychic relationship with these people and I can't let them down. I just want to see them well served by this. At this point it's like . . . Nancy is my sister.

> *Sid and Nancy used to go on £5 borrowing sprees at Virgin. They travelled everywhere in a taxi and would leave it running outside. They'd get as many fivers as they could and would then go and score some smack. Unlike other bands, the Pistols really frightened Warner Bros. They were really rude. They belittled people in satin tour jackets who wanted to congratulate them. They made big, important executives feel like shit.*

> AL

ABBE:
It's not absolutely my goal to crusade and campaign to make punks lovable. I personally think that the original punk movement was the best thing that has happened to culture in my lifetime. The idea that you could use rock 'n' roll, which has always been this rebellious thing, and be really FOCUSED

about it, like, let's dance to 'burn down the government' was a great feeling of power and a great release.

> *Nancy loved to perform. She loved to talk and act up. They were trying to talk me into shooting a porno scene for £100. But for punk moralistic reasons I didn't want to. 'Okay, fifty quid.' They tried really hard. They were incredibly pathetic and I felt like I was taking advantage of them just by being there.*
>
> LECH

ALEX:

Making the film took an emotional toll on people. It took a lot out of the actors to play those parts, both physically and mentally. It took a lot out if the crew as well. Week after week you'd watch these people systematically destroy themselves. You'd think, oh, it's just a film, no problem. But it is a problem. The mood on the set changed to a more sombre one when we stopped having fun in England and started getting dour and strange in the USA.

> *The weirdest night we ever played was the old Paradise Club in Soho. A strip club run by the Maltese mafia. We had to hose the stale cum off the seats. The gangsters and old hookers were there. We were more shocked by them than they were by us. Malcolm stood outside calling in the punters, pretending it still was a strip club.*
>
> ALAN

ABBE:

There is already a punk revival going on, but it is just a fashion thing. Like Live Aid, where you have this multi-million dollar production where guys are wheeled out of their air-conditioned trailers with catering and they go on stage for fifteen minutes and they think they've changed the world. I don't think this film or any one could change the world, but I hope that people will see it and realize that punks weren't monsters and also that Sid and Nancy weren't representative punks at all. They were really fucked up people and they would have been fucked up if they were living in New Jersey or in the suburbs. They would have been alcoholics feeding on each other; they would have crashed their car and died like that.

> *We all stood on the balcony and watched the ambulance take Nancy's body away. I remember looking around and everyone was stoned.*
>
> RITA

ALEX:

The thing you hear the most if you are a writer and you go to an American studio or a British production house with a good script is 'make the

10

characters more sympathetic' which means take away their tension, take away whatever makes them human. Have them behave in a sanitized, cardboard way and then maybe we'll make the picture. *Love Kills* was turned down by all the top production houses. If it weren't for Eric Fellner's herculean efforts and Margaret Matheson's faith and money the film would never have been made.

> *Everybody had a cat at that time in New York. Ian was a bus boy at Max's and he always had kittens. The girls would always take them. At every show there would be three or four girls with kittens in their pockets. Nancy's was called Smokey. She got it three months before she died. Its name changed all the time.*
>
> HEIDI

ABBE:
There is some kind of emotion and it is something they could never express, but could feel: they were in pain, they were angry, they were impotent, they were frustrated, but they had each other. There is always that kind of thing with youth. You know you are a gang and have a boyfriend and that makes you feel strong.

> *I don't think Sid needed fame. He was as famous in his mind when he did the pogo as when he did 'My Way'. He needed drugs and he needed Nancy.*
>
> DEBBIE

ALEX:
We shot *Love Kills* in London, Paris and the US in eleven weeks. The rough assembly lasted three hours fifty minutes. The finished film lasts less than two. What follows is the complete text of the film we shot. A lot of dialogue was invented by the actors. The published script is a composite of their dialogue and ours. This book is dedicated to everyone who gave us interviews or worked on the film.

> *By the end of the interview, Sid had really begun to depend on me. When I left he followed me to the top of the stairs and called out, 'Don't take the piss out of us, okay?' I wanted to hug him but I didn't.*
>
> ROSALIND

SID VICIOUS:
I hate films. It's pretence, it's lies, it's just shit. Like if you filmed a day in the life of me, for instance . . . that is the most boring thing on earth. It makes me sick to think that people will act out parts and, you know, like make it all seem larger than life, just so that some crud out there can get off on some fantasy: that life is wonderful and one day . . .

—————— —————— —————— —————— —————— ——————

CHELSEA HOTEL, ROOM 100, INTERIOR, DAY

Sid Vicious sits on a blood-stained bed. Tall, rail thin, bruised and pasty white. 21-years-old. Sid gazes towards the bathroom of the tiny room. The only window opens on to a ventilator shaft. The walls are dark. The floor is thick with garbage, black with blood.

> VOICE
> Who called 911?

A Fat Detective in a checkered vest sits down on a chair in front of Sid.

> DETECTIVE
> Did you call 911?
> **DID YOU CALL 911?**

There is no response from Sid. Nancy's body is zipped into a bag in the bathroom. Men load the bagged body on to a stretcher.

> DETECTIVE
> Get Sal in here. Keep the fucking press back, will ya?

The morgue men carry the body out. Sid's hands are cuffed behind his back and the detective moves him out of the room.

> DETECTIVE
> Let's go, kid.

CHELSEA HOTEL, HALLWAY, INTERIOR, DAY

Nancy's body passes through.

A punk girl, Gretchen, maybe 17, fishes in a huge purse looking for something she can't find. Upset, crying, stoned.

> GRETCHEN
> No way. Sid didn't do this.
> HE DIDN'T DO THIS . . . She was nice . . . She was . . .

A cop in a track suit studies a large portfolio. The book is full of loose and jumbled pictures — Nancy, platinum blonde, with various rock and roll luminaries. The hotel manager defends his reputation.

> MANAGER
> You know the type. I mean she was a camp follower. A camp
> follower. She would go to bed with anyone as long as they
> were part of a group. . .

The cop turns up a black and white photograph of Sid and Nancy.

Sid passes, handcuffed, with the detectives. He gives the manager an evil look.

> MANAGER
> Officer, please . . . We try to check everyone out as they come
> in . . . We can't be in charge of every single person.

―――――   ―――――   ―――――   ―――――   ―――――   ―――――

CHELSEA HOTEL, EXTERIOR, DAY

On the sidewalk reporters are clustering around a diminutive punkette. A video crew sets up.

> PUNKETTE
> I actually think it's kind of kool. I mean I liked her and
> everything, but it's just so kool Sid Vicious killed his girl-
> friend and she's DEAD!

The morgue men walk out of the hotel with the bagged body on the stretcher and load it into the back of the ambulance.

―――――   ―――――   ―――――   ―――――   ―――――   ―――――

CHELSEA HOTEL, LOBBY, INTERIOR, DAY

A reporter is trying to extract more information for his story from Alien Boy, a Chelsea resident.

> REPORTER
> Sid and Nancy. They were heroin addicts. Right?

> ALIEN BOY
> No, man. They didn't do any drugs. I knew 'em, man.

14

                    DESK CLERK
          We don't allow junkies in here. EVER.

Alien Boy puts his arm round the reporter and leads him away from the desk clerk.

                    ALIEN BOY
          Listen. Come here . . .
          Listen, I'm on my way down town. You got a couple of bucks?

                    REPORTER
          I don't have any money.

                    ALIEN BOY
          C'mon, man.

                    REPORTER
          It's my policy. I never do.

Sid, escorted by the two detectives, passes them.

                    ALIEN BOY
          Hey. Sid, man.

                    REPORTER
          That's Sid Vicious! *(following him)* That's Sid Vicious!

The walls are packed with grimy pop art. The residents — a mixed bunch of old people on walkers, artists, Europeans, dogs and wasted punks — back off as the detectives usher Sid through the lobby.

Suddenly flashbulbs start to pop.

                    REPORTERS
          There he is — Sid Vicious. Why'd you do it, Sid?

At the sight of the reporters, Sid's demeanour shifts. He sneers and stiffens, seems to grow in height. . .

> SID
> **FUCK OFF. I'll smash your fucking cameras.**

> DETECTIVE
> *(To reporters)* **Back off.**

The detectives shove Sid through the lobby doors. Flashbulbs.

—————— —————— —————— —————— —————— ——————

CHELSEA HOTEL, EXTERIOR, DAY

The detectives hustle Sid through a barrage of reporters on the pavement outside towards an unmarked police car.

> REPORTERS
> **Sid. Sid. Why'd ya do it, kid? Give us a statement. Give us a statement.**

The detectives shove Sid into the car. The door slams.

> REPORTERS
> **C'mon, Sid, smile for us. Why'd you do it?**

The morgue wagon takes off. The police car U-turns, heads in the opposite direction. We see Sid through the back window, watching the morgue wagon.

—————— —————— —————— —————— —————— ——————

INTERVIEW ROOM, INTERIOR, DAY

Sid Vicious sits on a stool under the lights. His shoes and belt have been taken away from him. He wears an open black shirt and black pants. Coming down from dope, shaking spasmodically, crying. Doors open and close. Cops wander in to check him out.

> BARNES
> **Where did you pick her up?**

> GREELEY
> **Why did you do it, kid?**

> McALPINE
> **How come the register says you were MARRIED?**

> GREELEY
> **Who was this chick, your groupie?**

> SID
> **NO!!!**

> McALPINE
> **Calm down, kid. Just tell us what's on your mind.**

BARNES
Just give us the facts about the corpse.

GREELEY
Yeah. We all know that she was a fucking whore. The bitch probably had it coming to her.

CHIEF
Get out of here, Greeley!

GREELEY
Chief, just give me five minutes alone with him.

CHIEF
I said GET OUT! What the hell you people think this is, a fuckin' METS GAME? Get OUT!

GREELEY
Fuck IT.

McALPINE
You made him mad, kid. You in big trouble.

GREELEY
I'll see you later, PUNK!

McALPINE
You in BIG trouble.

The chief slams the door behind Greeley. Pulls up a chair and straddles it in front of Sid.

CHIEF
Why so tense, kid? Look, we just want to know who the girl was . . . Where did you meet her? . . . Son? . . . *(Offers his cigarette.)* Son? . . .

Sid takes the cigarette. Snuffles. Takes a drag.

SID
I met her at Linda's.

CHIEF
Linda? Who's Linda?

———— ———— ———— ———— ———— ————

FLASHBACK SPRING 1977

TIMES SQUARE, EXTERIOR, DAY

Nancy Spungen, a compact blonde, in Spandex glitter gear, runs across the Square in hysterical tears. Make-up streaming.

17

TOPLESS BAR, INTERIOR, DAY

Trell, another blonde, and Gretchen sit at the bar of the seedy joint.

Nancy crashes in. Runs towards the ladies' room.

> MANAGER
> Hey, what time do you think you're on, sweetheart? Uh?

> TRELL
> *(Totally spaced)* Hey. Nancy.

Gretchen reaches out and grabs Nancy's arm.

> GRETCHEN
> Hey, Nancy. What's wrong?

> NANCY
> EVERYTHING. DUKE! He's gone. He just left.

> TRELL
> Who's gone?

> NANCY
> DUKE BOWMAN! My BOYFRIEND!

> GRETCHEN
> You remember, Trell. She met him at CBGB's last week.
> *(To Nancy)* What? What?

> TRELL
> Oh . . . yeah . . .

> NANCY
> I went by his place with . . . with these . . . these BROWNIES
> I made and . . . there was this other GIRL there and . . . and
> she said he went to . . . to ENGLAND.

> GRETCHEN
> England!

> TRELL
> Duke Bowman. He's the guy that plays that crazy glitter
> guitar . . .

> GRETCHEN
> *(To Trell)* Yeah. *(To Nancy)* You sure, Nance?

> NANCY
> Uh huh. He just LEFT. I'm so fucking STUPID! I wish I was
> dead.

> TRELL
> He's not gone . . . 's guitar's in the pawn shop. Down on . . .
> *(Forgets what she's saying.)*

The manager yells from the other end of the bar.

> MANAGER
>
> Hey! Nancy! Trell! Get up and dance. What do you think I'm paying you for, you fucking bimbos!

> GRETCHEN
>
> FUCK YOU! Nancy. Hey. Listen. Wait, I've got this idea. Why don't you go down the pawn shop and get his guitar and RESCUE it and take it back to England.

> NANCY
>
> *(Continuing to gulp and sob)* Oh right! How am I going to find him in ENGLAND!

> GRETCHEN
>
> England's real small. It's smaller than New York. Just go! Go! Nancy, stop crying.

> NANCY
>
> Are you trying to get rid of me?

> GRETCHEN
>
> No. Listen, just have a drink. Just go. Everything's gonna be cool. Really.

Nancy breaks into an insecure smile. Takes a sip of Gretchen's Kamikaze. The manager looms . . .

————— ————— ————— ————— ————— —————

LINDA'S PAD, INTERIOR, DAY

Spacious Georgian interior. Bay windows and expensive trim. Linda daubs the ends of cigarettes with drugs. Nancy sobs hysterically. Linda is 25, emaciated, short black crewcut.

> NANCY
>
> Only it wasn't cool at all! I came all the way from New York just to bring it to him. He just took it and he slammed the door in my face! He just pretended like he didn't even know who I was! I mean, he didn't even say thank you . . . We used to have this really great relationship . . .

(Passing the cigarette to Nancy.)

> LINDA
>
> I hate the smell of men. Ugh. They fucking smell. Ugh. Cunts!

> NANCY
>
> It's a real waste to smoke that shit. Don't you have any NEEDLES?

Linda passes the drugs back to Nancy who takes a long drag on the cigarette.

–––––– –––––– –––––– –––––– –––––– ––––––

BUCKINGHAM PALACE ROAD, EXTERIOR, DAY

Her Majesty's Royal Horse Guards trot past John and Sid. John is tall, hunched over, wears a long black coat over a checkered shirt, beer in hand. Sid is taller, with a black leather jacket and perpetual beer in hand. Pallid, spotty, devoid of bruises or track marks.

      SID
LINDAAAAAAAA!!!

      JOHN
LINDAAAAAAAA!!!

      SID
LINDAAAAAAAA!!!

No answer. Sid dislodges a chunk of broken paving stone . . .

–––––– –––––– –––––– –––––– –––––– ––––––

LINDA'S PAD, INTERIOR, DAY

Nancy exhales, lowers the cigarette. Pinpoint pupils.

      NANCY
Fuck him and his fucking guitar anyway. Right?

Crash. A paving stone flies through the window.

> LINDA
> I wonder who that is. *(She stands on the sofa and looks out.)*
> Naughty boys!

She tosses them her keys. Nancy rushes into the bathroom . . .

――――――― ――――――― ――――――― ――――――― ――――――― ―――――――

LINDA'S PAD, STAIRCASE, INTERIOR, DAY

John and Sid charge up the stately stairs. Sid bubbles with excitement.

> SID
> Think Linda's heard yet?

> JOHN
> I don't expect so, Sidney. It only happened ten minutes ago.
> Probably won't be on the news till six o'clock.

> SID
> What? You really think so? Think it'll be on telly?

――――――― ――――――― ――――――― ――――――― ――――――― ―――――――

LINDA'S PAD, INTERIOR, DAY

The sounds of Sid and John carry up the stairs. Linda unbolts the various locks and deadbolts. Mysterious straps hang from the back of the door. The door opens. Sid and John plough in. Sid flings his arms round Linda.

> SID
> Ey, Linda, guess what.

> LINDA
> What? You two got married.

> SID
> Nah. I'm the BASS PLAYER . . . *(kicks the wall)* . . . in the
> Osmonds!

> LINDA
> *(Spraying a mouthful of beer)* What happened to the other
> bloke?

> JOHN
> We fired him. He thought he was Paul McCartney. He washed
> his feet too much . . .

John and Linda walk through to the front room where Sid has pulled out a red spray can. Starts to graffiti SEX PISTOLS ARE GOD on the walls.

> JOHN
> . . . Sidney never washes his feet. WHAT'S FOR TEA?

LINDA
Baked beans or champagne.

JOHN
BOTH, please!

Linda hands John a plate of beans, which he starts devouring.

LINDA
How'd you like your beans, John?

JOHN
Oh they're wonderful! How old are they?

LINDA
A couple of weeks . . . and they've got cat shit in them.

Nancy enters, make-up readjusted. Looks worse than before. She watches Sid spraying the walls. Linda thrusts a half-eaten plate of beans at Sid.

LINDA
Nancy, this is Sid and John and they are . . .

NANCY
The SEX PISTOLS!! I LOVE the SEX PISTOLS! I have all your albums, back in New York.

JOHN
Oh yeah. Where's that then?

NANCY
(Turning to Sid) Hi, Johnny!

SID
I'm Sid. He's John.

NANCY
(To John) So, playing a gig tonight?

Sid sits down next to John with his plate of beans.

JOHN
'Playing a gig tonight.' Yeah, we're playing a gig tonight. So what.

NANCY
So I can come and check you out and see if you're as shit as
people say.

JOHN
We're worse. We're 'orrible.

*Linda starts opening another warm bottle of champagne. Sid grins and
drools beans.*

SID
Fuckin' great we are. Sex Pistols. Do yourself a favour.

JOHN
BORING Sidney! Boring! Boring! Boring! Boring! Boring!
(Makes a sound like a dalek, drools beans). Exterminate!
Exterminate!

SID
(Copies John) Exterminate! Exterminate!

BUCKINGHAM PALACE ROAD, EXTERIOR, DAY

An ancient Scottish laird emerges from his Rolls Royce. His chauffeur helps him into the building. John's and Sid's voices are heard as they come tramping up.

> SID
> Snow White and the Seven Dwarfs . . . and I really like Sleepy
> . . . and I like Dopey as well — he's really cool 'cos he's always
> stoned . . . Who's your favourite dwarf?

> JOHN
> Malcolm.

Sid sees a Scottie dog inside the Rolls Royce. Incensed, he walks towards the window of the car.

> SID
> . . . He's not a dwarf.

> JOHN
> He's a cunt! . . . DON'T, Sidney!

Sid pulls faces at the dog, with his nose pressed against the window.

> SID
> *(To dog)* Oy! *(To John)* 'Ere. Come here, John. Look!

> JOHN
> It's a doormat!

> SID
> No it's not. That's the chauffeur!

Sid scrambles on to the bonnet and starts spraying the window with the can of red paint.

> JOHN
> Who's got all the fuckin' money then? *(Twitchy but leading Sid on.)* This is fun!

Sid kicks the windscreen in.

> JOHN
> Kick it, Sid . . . Go on.

Sid starts pulling the broken windscreen away.

> JOHN
> Spray the beast, Sidney!

> SID
> Look at that!

> JOHN
> Go on, Sidney. Spray the beast!

Sid looks uncertainly at the dog. Starts making 'animal' noises.

> SID
> Oh. I really LIKE dogs.

> JOHN
> Oh, BORING.

> SID
> It's really sweet, that dog. *(More 'noises')* It's a really good
> dog.

Sid kicks the hood ornament away.

——————— ——————— ——————— ——————— ——————— ———————

PARADISE REVUE BAR, EXTERIOR, NIGHT

*Nancy and Linda cross the street, clad in their gig wear. Linda wears a
silver wig. The club is a former striptease joint. Malcolm stands outside
pretending that it still is.*

> MALCOLM
> Lovely girls, ten different girls. All nude, all the time. Step
> inside and have your fantasies fulfilled. *(To client)* Hello,
> sir. Take your clothes off and paint your body, all for the
> price of a drink. *(To Linda)* Good evening, boys. Would you
> like to step inside?

> LINDA
> *(Gruff voice)* 'Ere. These bints. They ain't FOREIGN, is they?

MALCOLM
No, sir. Every one an English rose. They grow on you.

Nancy and Linda groan and enter the club.

MALCOLM
(To the street) Here's the doorway to the seamy underbelly
of London. Step right up! . . . Fucking hell, is it worth it, I
ask myself? YES IT IS!

———— ———— ———— ———— ———— ————

PARADISE REVUE BAR, INTERIOR, NIGHT

*The band on stage plays 'O Bondage Up Yours'. John lurks among the old
hookers and Maltese gangsters at the bar. With him are supporters, Brenda,
Clive and Gloria. Clive is wearing a Cambridge Rapist mask. Sid is dancing.
Linda and Nancy buy cans of lager. Nancy takes a sip and grimaces.*

NANCY
Ugh. English beer tastes really WEIRD.

BRENDA
Na. Na. Don't drink that babe, 'cos Dexter buys all these cans
that are out of date . . .

NANCY
It's like PISS WATER.

BRENDA
Yeah, well, he buys em for ½p and then sells em for 50p.
It's well out of order.

John laughs. Nancy scowls. The gig ends.

NANCY
(Slapping John's back) Thanks for TELLING ME.

John ignores her. He watches Sid push his way through the crowd.

SID
(Arriving) 'Ere, John. You see me nut that hippy? Good 'ey?

*Phoebe arrives. Black, conservatively punk. Malcolm's secretary. She thrusts
a bass guitar into Sid's hands.*

PHOEBE
Oy. Oy. Look! Get up there and fulfil your contractual
obligation.

SID
(Inspecting guitar) Good God! What's this?

Sid starts for the stage. John grabs his arm.

JOHN
Ey, Sid. There's Dick Bent.

John indicates a journalist entering the club, Sid's good eye narrows.

SID
What shall I do?

JOHN
Exterminate!

SID
Exterminate!

Sid marches towards the offender. Phoebe sighs and John leers.

JOHN
Go, get him, Sidney. Go!

NANCY
Who's Dick Bent?

BRENDA
He's just some journalist who doesn't appreciate the Sex
Pistols.

Nancy watches Sid hit the reporter on the side of the head with his guitar. He falls down. Sid launches a flurry of kicks, none of which connect with him.

JOHN
Come on, Sidney! When you're ready!

SID
All right!

Sid heads for the stage. The Pistols launch into a ragged, white-noise version of 'Stepping Stone'. Sid's bass does not work. No problem. Nancy stands to the side of the stage watching Sid.

———— ———— ———— ———— ———— ————

LINDA'S PAD, INTERIOR, NIGHT

Bodies, mattresses and blankets on the floor. Several Pistols and the Bromley Contingent of Brenda, Clive, Olive, Abby, Polly, Smeggy and Bog Roll. Sid and John lie next to each other on the floor.

> SID
> You know I was so . . . I was so bored once that I fucked a dog!

> JOHN
> Oh, Sidney. How low can you get?

> SID
> . . . a corgi.

> JOHN
> One of the Queen's?!

> CLIVE
> Is it in yet?

> OLIVE
> No. Well, maybe . . .

Sid and John burp and belch, fart and laugh in the dark.

> ABBY
> Shut the fuck up!

A paper hits Sid in the face.

> SID
> Fuck off!

> ABBY
> Fuck you!

> SID
> . . . took me fuckin' eye out.

> ABBY
> Queer!

> SID
> *(To John)* I'm starving . . . I'm so hungry . . . I want a pizza!

> JOHN
> You are a fucking pizza.

28

SID
Bollocks.

Nancy appears beside them, removes her glitter top and several hundred-weight of jewellery. She climbs beneath the blankets next to John.

JOHN
You're not getting anythink.

NANCY
Why?

JOHN
You heard. Fuckin' Americans. That's all you ever think about. Sex. None of us fuck, see. Sex is ugly. None of your free hippie love shit here . . .

NANCY
You're insane.

She confiscates one of John's blankets.

JOHN
Gimme me blanket.

NANCY
Fuck off.

JOHN
(Moving off) LINDA!!

Nancy lays down on the mattress. Next to her is Sid's mop of tangled black hair and a long white back. She shivers and investigates it. Exaggerated snoring sounds are heard.

SID
(Muffled) Ugh, how vile. Sex is boring . . . ugly hippie shit.

NANCY
Jesus Christ! Fucking insane too . . . You're all fucking insane . . .

Nancy turns over, pulls the blankets tight around herself. Sid lays with one eye open, making snoring noises, terrified.

────── ────── ────── ────── ────── ──────

THE OLD MAHON, INTERIOR, DAY

All four Pistols lob handfuls of darts at the dart board. They are very drunk. It is lunchtime.

STEVE
Get the darts, Paul.

JOHN
Yeah, go on.

SID
Go on, Paul. Go on . . .

PAUL
Show me your hands . . . *(Backs towards the wall)* C'mon
both of 'em.

STEVE
Eh . . . get the darts!

PAUL
I'm watching you . . . you bastards . . . keep 'em where I can
see 'em.

PUBLICAN
Steady on, boys.

*Sid pretends to throw a dart at him. Paul cracks up. They all produce more
darts and hurl them at him.*

PAUL
Fuck off! Fuck off! Bastards! . . . It's not funny! You could
stick me in the eye . . . put it in me BRAIN! I couldn't play
the drums then.

JOHN
You can't play the fucking drums anyway!

PAUL
Bollocks!

JOHN
No you can't.

*Three of Duke Bowman's glitterati have entered the pub, accompanied
by members of the press.*

SID
'Ere. Talking of cunts who can't play!

The Pistols lob beermats and spit. John assumes a hunchback crouch, sits down scowling, slugging beer. Duke Bowman, the last of the longhairs to enter, is being interviewed by a reporter with Nancy close behind him.

STEVE
Hello girls! Where'd you get your perms?

DUKE
(Dimly) Er — fuck you, assholes!

The press spot the jocular and abusive Pistols and become excited.

NANCY
(Left alone with Duke) I don't mean to be mundane or anything, but I either need the drugs or the money . . . c'mon I'm broke — I need it — it's fifty pounds.

DUKE
FUCK YOU! Get the FUCK out!

He throws his beer in her face. Nancy is stunned, then mortified. Everyone watches her, except for the Press interviewing John. She rushes out. Sid moves.

PAUL
Four more pints, Sid!

Sid ignores him and exits past John and the press.

JOHN
No. I'm not a communist.

REPORTER
What do you think of Northern Ireland?

JOHN
It's all right where it is.

—————— —————— —————— —————— —————— ——————

THE OLD MAHON, EXTERIOR, DAY

Nancy is in tears, punching the wall. Sid emerges, watches her. Immediately she wipes her eyes, smearing her eyeliner.

SID
Are you all right?

NANCY
NO! Do I look all right! . . . The fucker in there ripped me off for fifty quid! Fucking scumbag . . .

She scrapes her knuckles up and down the wall.

SID

Wot, he stole it from your purse?

NANCY

Almost. I mean, I gave it to 'im the first night I was here. Scumbag! . . . why is it always like this? . . . cos I'm so FUCKING STUPID . . . it's embarrassing . . . *(She hits the wall again.)* He's a fuckin' junky anway. NEVER trust a junky!

SID

Wot, are they junkies, are they?

NANCY

Isn't everybody?

SID

You think you can get ME some?

NANCY

Maybe.

Sid eyes her bleeding hands and touches them.

SID

That looks like it hurts.

NANCY

It does.

SID

So does this.

Sid nuts the wall. Nancy is impressed.

NANCY

You really want some?

SID

Yeah.

NANCY

Give me all your money. *(Sid produces crumpled bills and change.)* I'll be back in an hour.

Nancy runs for the bus and jumps aboard. Sid stands outside the Old Mahon.

SID

See you here! . . . In the pub!

——— ——— ——— ——— ——— ———

HOTEL ROOM, INTERIOR, DAY

Nancy sits on the edge of a twin bed. Rock Head, a down and dirty US rocker, no shirt, leather pants, heavy mascara, is drying his hair with a blow-dryer.

NANCY
You look great.

ROCK
Yeah. I know.

NANCY
So . . .

ROCK
You understand I don't sell normally. . . *(He takes a bible from a drawer. It's full of fixing tools and little bags. Revolution on TV)*. . . This is all for personal consumption.

NANCY
You can't do all that by yourself.

ROCK
Hey, man. The pressures of the road. I guess I don't have to tell you about that, Nancy. Whether it's sex or dope or stamp collecting, you got to have that sideways pressure valve.

NANCY
You look great.

ROCK
Right!

NANCY
Can I have two dimes?

ROCK
TWO? Uh, gee, I don't know. These are BIG DIMES. I'm really shafting myself letting go of even one.

NANCY
Oh, come on, Rock. For old times' sake.

ROCK
Old times, hmm? Nancy, that's sweet.

NANCY
So how about it?

ROCK
I'll sell you two for one if you'll fuck me and split one right now. Deal?

Nancy considers several options.

NANCY
Deal.

———   ———   ———   ———   ———   ———

THE OLD MAHON, EXTERIOR, NIGHT

It's raining. Sid Vicious waits stoically seated on the pavement by the entrance to the pub. Sid's friend Wally arrives. Just as Sid takes his cues from John, Wally takes his cues from Sid. He has spiky black hair and a motorcycle jacket with Wally written on the back. He is soaked through.

> WALLY
> Sid. Coming for a pint?

> SID
> Nah. I'm waitin' for this bird.

> WALLY
> Fuckin' A. What's her name?

> SID
> Nancy.

> WALLY
> Nancy. You mean that American bird? The junky?

> SID
> She ain't a junky.

> WALLY
> Friend of Linda's? Been staying over there? Nancy. She's a junky.

> SID
> Yeah, well anyway. I'm waitin' for her.

Wally shakes his head. He puts an arm around Sid's shoulder, pulls him into the pub.

> LANDLORD
> Let's have your glasses please!

———— ———— ———— ———— ———— ————

THE SPICE OF LIFE, EXTERIOR, DAY

Sid and Wally reel out of another boozer. Wally wears a bright red leather jacket and has bright red hair. Rich kid. Sid has his usual clobber on.

> SID
> . . . so the next thing I know, there's these three big Rastas towerin' over me and Wobble's nowhere to be seen. One of 'em says, you lookin' for trouble, mon? and I say, FUCKIN' YEAH! and then . . .

> WALLY
> Really? Is this really true?

SID
YEAH! I think so . . .

——————— ——————— ——————— ——————— ——————— ——————— ———————

BERWICK STREET MARKET, EXTERIOR, DAY

Sid and Wally are walking through the market.

WALLY
. . . I'm thinking of starting up this club where you can, like,
drink after hours or in the afternoon.

SID
Yeah, what you gonna call it?

WALLY
'Wally's Gaff'.

SID
That's really good, that. Must have taken you ages to think
that up.

WALLY
Well, it's got a certain ring of street cred about it, don't you
think?

SID
(Northern accent) Oh, let's all go to Wally's Gaff and have a
lager!

WALLY
Two pounds fifty!

SID
Pink gin?

WALLY
That's a fiver!

SID
Coca-cola?

WALLY
Seven pounds and forty nine pence!

SID
Water?

WALLY
Twelve pounds fifty.

SID
And where you gonna get all the money for this?

WALLY
I told you I'm getting a mortgage from, like, the Abbey
National, or somewhere.

As Wally and Sid plod unsteadily along, a gold Cadillac stretch limo with blacked out windows cruises past.

WALLY
Rod Stewart at two o' clock. *(They both aim imaginary machine guns)* Bubbadabubbadabubbadabubbadam! Oy! You wankers!

———   ———   ———   ———   ———   ———

CADILLAC, INTERIOR, DAY

Sid and Wally run along behind, throwing things. Nancy sits in the back with Rock Head and his new girlfriend Hermione. Rock is strung out and mean. Nancy's eyeliner has run.

ROCK
(Slamming his fist into his palm) Go through that door and climb to the top of the stairs. Don't speak to anyone. Ask for Asrhaf. Don't let her keep you waiting.

The Cadillac pulls up.

NANCY
Why do I have to go? I've got a broken heel.

Hermione reaches across and opens the door next to Nancy.

HERMIONE
And don't get BURNED!

———   ———   ———   ———   ———   ———

SOHO, EXTERIOR, DAY

Nancy limps on one stiletto heel into the building.

———   ———   ———   ———   ———   ———

CADILLAC, INTERIOR, DAY

Rock lies catatonic in the back seat, rhythmically slamming a clenched fist into his other palm.

ROCK
I hate . . . to wait . . .

Sirens. A white Police Jag hurtles round the corner and can't get past them.

ROCK
GET ME OUT OF HERE!

The chauffeur puts his foot down. Hermione eyes Nancy's holdall and bags.

> HERMIONE
> What about that chick's gear?

> ROCK
> **JETTISON!**

———— ———— ———— ———— ———— ————

SOHO, EXTERIOR, DAY

Nancy's stuff is flung out of the back door. Sid and Wally turn the corner as the Cadillac takes off.

> WALLY
> *(To the disappearing vehicle.)* **Rod!**

> SID
> **All right, Rod!**

Sid and Wally start rummaging through Nancy's clothes. Sid finds some knickers, sniffs them and puts them on Wally's head.

> **'Ere you are! They're your Mum's!**

Nancy stumbles one-heeled down the stairs. She sees her belongings and starts running towards them.

> NANCY
> **SHIT! MOTHERFUCKERS! My CLOTHES!** *(Starts picking up her things.)*

> SID
> **'Ere you. Where's my money?**

> NANCY
> **Shit! Goddamn!**

> SID
> **Look . . .**

> NANCY
> *(To Wally)* **HELP ME!**

> SID
> **I gave you some money the other day. What about my money?**

> NANCY
> **Shut up and help me . . .**

> SID
> **Nobody fucks with me, see. I oughta smash your face in. Listen! LISTEN, what about my DRUGS.**

NANCY
Here.

She thrusts a package into Sid's hands and continues gathering up her things. Sid sits down on the pavement and starts to open it at once.

NANCY
You can't run drugs on the sidewalk, Johnny. What are you an IDIOT?

SID
I'm Sid . . .

WALLY
(Brightly) Do you wanna use my gaff?

NANCY
What's a gaff?

WALLY
Me house . . . *(American accent)* me apartment.

SID
(Laughs) He's a club owner!

———— ———— ———— ———— ———— ————

CLISSOLD ROAD, EXTERIOR, DUSK

Nancy, Sid and Wally have jumped off the 73 bus and are marching briskly up the road. Schoolchildren smash up a Ford Capri with hockey sticks. Nice neighbourhood.

SID
Where's the fish and chips?

WALLY
What fish and chips?

SID
The fish and chips you promised to buy us.

NANCY
Look, why don't we just go in. You can do that later.

SID
We will. He lets us in, we do the drugs, he goes and gets the fish and chips.

WALLY
But I want to do some of the drugs.

SID
Yeah, you will . . . We'll save you some . . .

WALLY

Cheers! *(Opens the gate to a terraced house)* This is where
the bouncers are going to stand.

WALLY'S PAD, INTERIOR, DUSK

*The top floor flat. Wally is a very tidy boy. He has pictures of Marc Bolan
and the Pistols on his walls. He also has a guinea pig named Martin. Wally is
rockin' out on his guitar. He and Sid look on intently as Nancy shoots up.*

NANCY

. . . like I was at CBGB's at this audition, right? So this guy
says can you sing like Debbie Harry? That shithead. Listen,
it's a bad deal looking like an established star, let me tell you.

*(She draws the liquid dope out of the spoon. Everything is intensely clean and
gleaming.)* I mean, I like Debbie. We're really good friends, actually.

NANCY

You've done this before, right?

SID

Oh, yeah . . . yeah.

NANCY

Good veins.

BATHROOM, INTERIOR, NIGHT

*Sid convulses on the bathroom floor. Nancy bends over him, wipes puke off
his mouth. Wally watches, spaced.*

*Outside, the clattering rumble of trains on the North London Line. Yellow
coachlights strobe across them.*

BEDROOM, INTERIOR, NIGHT

*Sid and Nancy make love. Wally lies on the floor, totally spaced, playing
with two toy cars.*

BEDROOM, INTERIOR, EARLY MORNING

Outside, it is getting light. Nancy looks at Sid, begins gathering her things.

SID
Where're you going?

NANCY
Well...

SID
What?

NANCY
Don't you want me to?

SID
No.

Nancy looks at Sid again. There is no misunderstanding. She turns over and they embrace.

————   ————   ————   ————   ————

RECORDING STUDIO, INTERIOR, NIGHT

Steve tries to teach Sid a bass line. Brenda is bandaging John's face. Sid tries to sing the chorus at the same time.

SID
We don't fuckin' care!

JOHN
No! There's no fuckin' — get the words right! Ow! Be careful!

STEVE
You got four strings on the bass, Sid. One, two, three, four...

High heels clatter down the stairs. Nancy enters wearing a rubber mac and anarchy armbands. Her arms are full of parcels and takeaway food.

SID

And we don't care!

NANCY

Pizza time!

SID

Pizza, my favourite food!

Sid drops the bass immediately. He embraces Nancy.

NANCY

So what are you waiting for? Playback? How many tracks have you laid?

PAUL

None. We ain't done no songs either.

ABBY

Sid's still learning it.

NANCY

Sid! What are you doing?

SID

I'm eating!

Nancy pulls the pizza from Sid's mouth. Steve and Paul are having fun with the bananas.

NANCY

No! You can't have any pizza until you've finished at least one song.

SID

Aw! Fuck off!

NANCY

No! I'm serious! What are you doing here? You're in the studio . . . these places cost like fifty grand a minute. You could be SHININ' OUT, but what! . . . you're just wonking off!

JOHN

Wanking!

NANCY

What happened to you? Did you try and kiss your mother?

JOHN

It's none of yer business.

BRENDA
John got beaten up by fascists.

OLIVE
Five minutes to last orders! I'm going to get pissed!

An exodus starts.

NANCY
Want some pizza, Johnny?

STEVE & PAUL
(Imitating Nancy) 'Want some pizza, Johnny'!!!

JOHN
I don't like pizza.

BRENDA
(Leaving) He doesn't like to be called Johnny. Likes to be called John.

SID
See yer, Johnny!

PAUL
Fuckin' cabbies, that's what we should be. Make 200 quid a night bein' a cabby. . .

SID
Why don't you fuck off and be one then?

PAUL
'Cos it takes eighteen months to learn.

SID
. . . and you need a driving licence, too.

PAUL
. . . and a set of golf clubs.

Steve and Paul leave.

NANCY
(Alone with Sid) I don't think Johnny likes me.

SID
He doesn't like anyone. He's a fool.

NANCY
You like me, don't you? *(Sid nods. They embrace.)*
Kiss my toes.

SID
You want me to?

Sid drops down before her; pulls off her boots and rips away her stockings. Deliberate and sensuous, he starts to kiss her toes.

42

THE SILVERY THAMES, EXTERIOR, DAY

Seen from above, a bulky pleasure boat, the Queen Elizabeth, parts the waters. The deck is packed with reporters and punks. National Anthem plays.

—————— —————— —————— —————— ——————

QUEEN ELIZABETH, EXTERIOR, DAY

Malcolm squeezes through the crowd with Paul in tow. He's trying to round up members of the band. As fast as he can find one, another disappears. Wally, Clive and co. are tossing lifebelts overboard. Malcolm and Phoebe have moved into the top cabin.

> PHOEBE
> John's in the lav, Malc. Seasick.

> MALCOLM
> Seasick? Why can't he puke over the side? That's why we have photographers . . . we need an explosion! . . . Where are you going, Sidney?

> SID
> Oh, Malkie-walkie, gimme some money . . .

> MALCOLM
> Sidney, as a Sex Pistol, all your human needs are seen to — food, beer, designer wardrobe. Why do you need money?

> SID
> Uh, I don't know . . . little things . . . around the house.

> MALCOLM
> What sort of little things? What are these bruises on your arm?

43

SID
I fell over . . .

PHOEBE
Look. Leave him alone!

SID
(Moving off) Bollocks, you wanker! *(Shouts)* This man is violent! Get out of my way . . . Nancy!! . . . yum, yums!

————— ————— ————— ————— ————— —————

BOAT CORRIDOR, INTERIOR, DAY

Sid stumbles downstairs as John staggers from the bog.

SID
Ey, John. I've had a really good idea!

JOHN
What?

SID
I'm gonna get a tattoo on my head.

JOHN
Oh, what's it going to say?

SID
(Thumping his head) It's going to say Brain Damage!

STEVE
(Thrusting a banana into Sid's mouth) 'Ere you are, Sid. Get a load of that!

————— ————— ————— ————— ————— —————

BELOW DECKS, INTERIOR, DAY

A chocolate-eating orgy in progress in the bar. A videotape of the notorious Bill Grundy interview plays. Sid's mum is surrounded by reporters. Olive is passed out on the floor.

Sid arrives, clambering over the tables, handing out cans of beer.

SID
It's Christmas time you minions! Here you go! *(Sits between Nancy and Brenda)* Here I am!

Sid playfully pretends to strangle Nancy. Brenda tries to fit earrings in his ear. Journalists mill around.

REPORTER
Is this your girlfriend, Sid?

SID
What one?

Sid pretends to bang their heads together.

NANCY
We both are!

BRENDA
We love him!

NANCY
We love Sid and the Sex Pistols!

BRENDA
You gonna give us any money for this? . . . fucking Dylan.

ABBY
(Slurping from a bottle of champagne) Think of a name
for my baby?

BRENDA
Bastard.

ABBY
. . . I got a rat called Bastard.

*Nancy presents Sid with a gaily wrapped box. He tears it open and pulls
out a padlock and chain. Nancy hangs it around his neck and clicks the lock.*

SID
Hey, that's really cool . . . where's the key?

NANCY
What key?

SID
Hahahahahahaha

REPORTER
Your mum says you're a nice boy, Sid. Any comment?

NANCY
(Twisting Sid's collar) He's not a nice boy. He's the meanest
bastard that ever walked the fucking earth! *(Withering look
from Sid's mum.)* I wish MY mom was here. My mom's
REAL supportive of ME!

PHOEBE
Sid! Malcolm wants you upstairs. *(No response.)* Sid! Hey,
STUPID!

SID
What?

NANCY
(*Cuffing him*) Don't answer to 'Stupid'.

PHOEBE
Sid. Upstairs.

NANCY
Why?

PHOEBE
WHAT?

NANCY
Why? It's gonna rain. You'll get electrocuted. No one's gonna listen anyway.

PHOEBE
Who the FUCK are you, anyway?

NANCY
Nancy Spungen.

Sid grins and then immediately feels guilty.

SID
S'pose I'd better go . . .

Nancy plants a big kiss on his lips. She musses his carefully spiked 'do.'

SID
Oh, no! Not my hair! Bloody hell!

Sid gets up to leave, closely followed by Nancy.

NANCY
I'll fix it . . . I'll fix it . . .

Abby continues to spray champagne over Brenda.

SID'S MUM
(*To reporters*) I think it's awful, them being beaten up like that. I mean, you know, they're REALLY nice boys. And anyway, I thought this was meant to be a free country, yeah? I mean, look, I remember Simon – Sid, I mean – when he was a little boy, I mean, he couldn't go anywhere without me . . .

━━━━━ ━━━━━ ━━━━━ ━━━━━ ━━━━━ ━━━━━ ━━━

QUEEN ELIZABETH, EXTERIOR, DUSK

John, Steve and Paul attempt 'Anarchy in the UK'. Feedback from John's mike drowns out his voice.

Police start closing in.

JOHN
I didn't know PIGS could SWIM!

GENTS, INTERIOR, DUSK

Sid tries to tease his hair back into spikes. Nancy helps him with a variety of products including egg whites and chip fat. Above deck, the band is heard.

NANCY

But, Sid, I love your hair . . .

SID

It takes ages to make it stick up properly . . .

NANCY

(Shoving her hands down his pants) **Make WHAT stick up properly?**

SID

NANCY . . . Look, I'm supposed . . . to be . . . upstairs . . .

They kiss. Fall out of sight beneath the wash basin.

NANCY

Well then, go upstairs . . .

——— ——— ——— ——— ——— ———

DOCK, EXTERIOR, NIGHT, MAJOR FIGHTING

A mass of punks flee. Drunk reporters stagger and fall, ignoring the deranged cops dragging women by their legs and hair.

Unnoticed, Sid and Nancy stumble down the gangplank. Wrapped around each other they cruise through the chaos and away.

——— ——— ——— ——— ——— ———

LINDA'S PAD, INTERIOR, DAY

Nancy lies in Linda's pink fur-lined bedroom She is sick and shivering. Sid strokes her hair. Linda struggles into a rubber bondage harness, listening to the phone. No one there. She hangs up and pulls on a floral print silk dress.

LINDA

Nobody there. I've got to go, Sid. Appointment at the House of Lords.

SID

What about Nancy? Should I make her a cup of tea?

LINDA

Cup of tea won't make a difference, Sid. You've got to come up with some money and get her some smack.

SID

How am I supposed to do that? Maybe she just needs some sleep.

LINDA

Sid. It's not a hangover. She can't sleep it off. If you don't get her something, she'll get sicker and sicker . . .

Linda exits, stuffing a whip in her purse. Nancy groans loudly.

NANCY

My BONES hurt . . .

Sid gets up — sits down — gets up again.

SID

Oh shit . . .

———— ———— ———— ———— ———— ————

PHONE BOX, INTERIOR, NIGHT

Nancy, sickly and crying, is on the phone. Sid smokes a cigarette.

NANCY

(Shouting) Guess what, Mom? We got MARRIED! Me and SID! SID VICIOUS, you remember from the Sex Pistols! Yeah . . .

SID

Hello, Mom! Hello, Mom!

NANCY

Yeah, we did it. No, I'm not pregnant! We did it 'cause we love each other. We're really IN LOVE! . . . it's great . . . yeah you'll love him, too. He's so sweet. He's nothing like the papers say. Uh huh, yeah . . . So, so anyway, why don't you send us a WEDDING PRESENT for our HONEYMOON? . . . No, we don't need any sheets . . . Why don't you send us some MONEY? . . . Well, it's early there, right? So you could go to American Express, like, RIGHT NOW, before it closes and send us two hundred dollars and then Sid could go and pick it up tomorrow, like, first thing when they open . . . Why NOT? I am SO married! I AM! What do you mean? . . . HE LOVES ME MORE THAN YOU DO! Yes, I AM! . . . NO! Shut up! Listen to me! IF YOU DON'T SEND US SOME MONEY RIGHT NOW, WE'RE BOTH GONNA FUCKIN' DIE! FUCK YOU!!

Nancy slams the phone down and freaks out, bashing her fists against the glass. Two windows break. Sid tries to restrain her. Eyes glazed, rigid, hyperventilating, Nancy falls out of the phone box.

NANCY
I fucking hate them! I fucking hate them! FUCKERS!
MOTHER FUCKERS! They wouldn't send us ANY MONEY!
They said we'd spend it on DRUGS!

SID
Yeah, well, we would . . .

NANCY
It doesn't matter. They don't CARE. My own family doesn't
trust me. They hate me. My own family hates me.

SID
I love you. Look, come here, your hand's bleeding.

NANCY
GOOD!

_____ _____ _____ _____ _____ _____

LEAFY LANE, EXTERIOR, DAY

A windowless van drives through the freezing countryside

_____ _____ _____ _____ _____ _____

VAN, INTERIOR, DAY

*Sid and Nancy are being interviewed. Steve is the only other Pistol present.
He makes out with a tall Swedish girl. Sid seems to be on the nod. It's
Nancy's first interview and she is being very cooperative with the reporter.*

NANCY
I left home when I was like 11. When I was 15, I was livin' in
New York. I was an exotic dancer. That's like with no clothes
on. Sid didn't know anything about sex before he met me.
The first time we screwed he wet the bed. But now I think he
has sort of a sexual 'aura'. That's 'cause of me.

49

JOURNALIST
Are you a groupie, Nancy?

Nancy frowns. Sid wakes up for a second.

SID
Nancy's not a groupie. Nancy . . . is . . . *(Drifts off again.)*

NANCY
(Kissing him) Thank you, Sid . . . Oh, tell them about Henry
Green . . . yeah . . .

SID
. . . Hughie Green — he's the most disgusting . . .

NANCY
Yeah!

SID
. . . person . . .

NANCY
Yeah!

SID
I hate the — whole public . . .

NANCY
Yeah!

SID
. . . they're a load of shits . . .

NANCY
Write this down! It's IMPORTANT!

SID
. . . you get on the streets — and you can print that —

NANCY
Yeah!

———— ———— ———— ———— ———— ————

UXBRIDGE COLLEGE, EXTERIOR, NIGHT

A concrete bunker vibrates to the sounds of 'No Feelings'.

———— ———— ———— ———— ———— ————

UXBRIDGE COLLEGE, INTERIOR, NIGHT

*A huge gymnasium packed with punks. The Pistols perform. Awful acoustics.
Sid does his best to keep up.*

BRENDA
I'M BORED! I could be down the Old Red Lion tonight — pulling!

OLIVE
Punks don't go out pulling! They go to fucking boring gigs like this. That's what it's all about!

ABBY
(Holding a baby with a tiny green Mohican) We eat babies. Don't we, Bastard?

CLIVE
I ain't going to be a punk no more.

BRENDA
What you gonna be then, Clive? A SKINHEAD?

CLIVE
I'm gonna be a Rude Boy like my Dad.

The song ends. Immediately, Sid gets accosted by a Ted. A small brawl ensues.

MALCOLM
(Observing from the balcony) Phoebe. How would you like to supervise our Sidney for a month or two?

PHOEBE

No way.

MALCOLM

Go on. You'd be a good influence on the boy. Why not?

PHOEBE

Infectious hepatitis. Loony girlfriend. Drugs.

MALCOLM

Boys will be boys.

PHOEBE

It's time he went back to his mum's.

MALCOLM

Mmmm . . .

———— ———— ———— ———— ———— ————

SID'S MUM'S HOUSE, INTERIOR, DAY

Framed photograph of Dennis Hopper and the other guy in **Easy Rider,** *astride their motorbikes. Lace curtains, bullfighting posters, antique hippie gear, several television sets in boxes, morotcycle engine on a table in the lounge. Nancy watches the test card on TV, wearing a pair of acid flashback glasses.*

SID

Fuck. Fuck it. FuckfuckFUCK IT!

NANCY

What? What's the matter?

SID

Can't find it! My ACTION MAN!

NANCY

You mean G.I. Joe?

SID

I only had it in my hand five minutes ago. I've had it since I was a kid! WANT TO KILL!!

Nancy finds Action Man beneath a mangled item of clothing. She picks it up and tosses it at Sid.

NANCY

Wait! Flying in! Telly Savalas!

The male war doll lands in the sink among the filthy dishes.

SID

(Makes dramatic drowning sounds) **Oh no. Aaah, he's drowning!** *(American accent)* **I tried to save him — but it's**

52

too late!

NANCY

I used to have a SPECIAL HAIR BARBIE.

SID

You mean, Cindy, Nancy.

NANCY

No. I mean Barbie, Sidney. I'll never look like Barbie —
Barbie doesn't have bruises. Sid! Look at this! I look disgusting!

SID

Look, Nancy. Why don't you do these dishes, please, eh?

NANCY

WHAT? WHAT DID YOU SAY TO ME?

SID

Fuck it. I'll do 'em myself.

NANCY

Good! What's the matter, Sid? You do a little SPEED or
something?

SID

(Spazzing out) Nah. Well, yeah. Only a bit though. I was
bored. I'm bored now. Where's the bloody soap?

NANCY

Up your ass.

Sid starts washing the dishes with cold water and spit. Nancy stubs her
cigarette out in a Grecian column ashtray then tips the ashtray on the floor.

NANCY

Ohh! I better cover this up before someone sees it.

Sid grabs an enormous Hoover and starts trundling it back and forth across
the floor.

SID

Shit! Christ! Look my mum's gonna be home soon! Stop
mucking about!

NANCY

Oh, what's the difference?

SID

(Shouting above the vacuum) Yeah, well. It's the least I
can do! What with her RISKING HER LIFE every day
WORKING as a MOTORCYCLE MESSENGER!

NANCY

Oh God. IF YOU WERE EARNING HALF OF WHAT

YOU'RE WORTH, YOU COULD AFFORD TO BUY YOUR
MOM A HARLEY! YOU PRICK! *(She stamps out of the
room.)*

SID
WHY DON'T YOU SHUT YOUR FUCKING MOUTH!
IF IT WEREN'T FOR ME MUM'S KINDNESS WE'D BE ON
THE FUCKING STREETS!

——————— ——————— ——————— ——————— ——————— ———————

MUM'S BEDROOM, INTERIOR, DAY

*Sid pushes the vacuum past the bedroom door. He looks aghast at Nancy
who has donned an exaggerated hippie outfit and is jumping up and down
on his mum's bed.*

NANCY
AND IF IT WEREN'T FOR YOUR OWN STUPIDITY WE'D
BE LIVING IN OUR OWN APARTMENT IN PARIS!
FRANCE!

SID
Get off the fucking bed!

NANCY
NO! Look at this shit. Can you believe this! YEEAACH!!

SID
Look. OK. Look, stop it now. We've had the fun. Now,
take that off — it's my mummy's. Look, it'll tear!

NANCY
Oh really? I thought it was yours.

Sid slaps her across the face.

NANCY
(Eyes full of tears) OK, scumbag, I'm not living here anymore.
Fuckhead! *(She rushes out.)*

SID
Nancy . . . NANCY!!!

——————— ——————— ——————— ——————— ——————— ———————

STREET, EXTERIOR, DAY

*Nancy is running down the road carrying her holdall and Harrods bags. Sid
pursues her in his underpants.*

NANCY
FUCK YOU!

54

SID

FINE! Piss off when the GOING GETS TOUGH! Insult me ONLY FUCKING MOTHER!

NANCY

FUCK BOTH OF YOU! YOU LOVE HER MORE THAN ME!

Ma Vicious rolls past on her Honda 750.

MUM

(Shouts) **Hi, son!**

SID

(Still in pursuit) **YEAH, I FUCKING DO AND ALL!**

NANCY

Mother's boy! You asshole! *(Stops in front of a shop window)* **Aaaghhh!** . . . **Sid! Sid! I look like fucking Stevie Nicks in hippie clothes!** . . . **Aaghh!**

SID

No. You look nice . . . you look nice —

NANCY

(Pulling all her clothes off) **Oh, YUK!** . . . **Help me!** . . . **SHIT!**

Nancy gets changed in the street, pulling new items from the Harrods bags. Laughing, Sid picks up the discarded clothes. Nancy laughs too.

———— ———— ———— ———— ———— ————

LINDA'S PAD, INTERIOR, DAY

John enters. He sees a frightened-looking middle-aged man hanging from manacles on the ceiling. Linda is drinking champagne from a half-pint beer mug.

LINDA
(Surprised) Hello, John! What are you doing up so early in the afternoon?

JOHN
Come to see me best mate.

LINDA
(Indicating the kitchen) He's in his boudoir.

JOHN
Oh. Is he out of it? *(She nods.)* Eh, Linda. You know you got a naked man hanging from your ceiling.

LINDA
Oh, don't mind him. He's one of my customers. Edward. Just abuse him now and then and he'll be as good as gold.

EDWARD
(Whining, refined) Don't hurt me . . . for God's sake, don't hurt me . . . I'll do anything you want — but I implore you not to hurt me . . . please.

JOHN
SHADAAAP!!!

Linda laughs.

━━━━━ ━━━━━ ━━━━━ ━━━━━ ━━━━━ ━━━━━

KITCHEN, INTERIOR, DAY

Black Label crates and much graffiti. Painting of a noble horse in the sink. Mattress, TV set and Nancy's bags.
Sid and Nancy have fallen asleep fucking. Sid's body is dead weight on hers. He snores. She wheezes.

JOHN
Sid. Sidney. Sid. Wakey-wakey! Rise and shine! Come on. Sid, wake up dear! SIDNEY, wake up! *(Kicks him.)*

SID
Fuckin' stop it. . .

JOHN
I'm surprised you can even FEEL IT!

NANCY
Leave us alone. . .

JOHN
I'm sorry I kicked you, Sidney. It was an accident . . . you ought to get out more. It STINKS in here. Look, I've got two tickets to see ROCK HEAD at the Rainbow — it'll do

you good to go and see him. I hear he's cleaned up his act, doesn't do ANY drugs or drink at all, hardly . . . *(To Nancy)* and he's all the better for it!

NANCY
I KNOW Rock Head.

JOHN
I bet you do. C'mon, Sidney, let's go.

NANCY
(Licking Sid's ear) Rock Head's got the BEST drugs.

SID
Let's go see Rock Head! . . . 'Ere John, boy. Do us a favour. Make us a cup o' tea!

------- ------- ------- ------- ------- -------

HOTEL IN BELGRAVIA, EXTERIOR, DAY

Nancy marches towards the venerable hotel, carrying a cap pistol, pursued by stumbling Sid and recalcitrant John. Sid wears a Ken-doll cowboy suit and carries two pistols.

JOHN
Super uncool, this is. Fuckin' stupid groupie stuff. I don't even want to be here.

Sid and Nancy lark about as they approach the door of the hotel.

------- ------- ------- ------- ------- -------

HOTEL RECEPTION, INTERIOR, DAY

Nancy bangs on the reception desk.

NANCY
The Sex Pistols for Mister Head!!

RECEPTIONIST
(Picking up the phone) Mr Head's room, please.

SID
COR! Worra fuckin' palace! I wish I lived here. *(Falls down)*

JOHN
(To receptionist) What are you looking at, toerag?

------- ------- ------- ------- ------- -------

ROCK HEAD'S SUITE, INTERIOR, DAY

Rock's uptown groupie opens the door. Present are Rock's trainer, Rock's business manager and Rock's secretary. The groupie and secretary both wear Chanel suits and a rose Rock has given them.

NANCY
ROCK!!! You Big Head!!!

ROCK
Hi, ah . . . Peggy, isn't it?

NANCY
NANCY! And this is Sid Vicious and Johnny. They're from the Sex Pistols. IMPRESS them with your DRUGS.

ROCK
Drugs? Do we have any drugs, boys?

TRAINER
Rock Head does not DO drugs.

NANCY
Right. Don't be so fucking stingy. Get out the drawer — we'll have a Bible reading!

SID
(To trainer) Give me five pounds!

TRAINER
Fuck off!

Sid and Nancy flop on to a love seat and begin pelting everyone with sugared almonds.

ROCK
Eh, look. You want water? I've got some with bubbles in it.

JOHN
How about some ROOM SERVICE, Mr Head. *(An almond hits him.)* Fuck off!

ROCK
. . . Ah, Jennifer. Ring for the cart.

NANCY
Fuck him, Sidney. His drugs were garbage, anyway . . .

ROCK
They were NOT!

SID
(To manager) Lend us five pounds.

JENNIFER
(Fake French accent) . . . Allo? Room service? . . .

———— ———— ———— ———— ———— ————

ROCK HEAD'S SUITE, INTERIOR, LATER

Rock Head on his exercycle. John lies on the love seat. Sid and Nancy go at it on the bed. John chugs Jack Daniels. Rock sips Perrier.

ROCK

(Pedalling) So. It appears we are related.

JOHN

Eh?

ROCK

The press. They call me the BIG DADDY OF PUNK. Your ROLE MODEL. *(Glancing at Sid and Nancy)* Lovely couple.

JOHN

FUCK YOU, ROCK HEAD! What the FUCK are you doing in a place like this, anyway? None of us would EVER be CAUGHT DEAD here in a fuckin' hotel like this — HOTEL DE POUFTEURS!

ROCK

Hey, cool out, dude. I paid my dues . . .

JOHN

Yeah! and I paid seven quid to see you! Here! I'd rather fuckin' PUKE! *(Storms off.)*

———————— ———————— ———————— ———————— ———————— ————————

HOTEL BATHROOM, INTERIOR, EVENING

Rock finds John raging up and down, overturning T'ang Dynasty vases, streaming angry tears . . .

JOHN

BORING! OLD! FART! PATHETIC! DISCO! WANKER!

ROCK

You didn't like the show. I didn't like the show either. What can I say? Here's seven pounds. Take it.

JOHN

(Rages on and throws money back.) Fuck you and your seven pounds!

ROCK

What's the matter with you?

JOHN

YOU'RE THE MATTER!!! You're FULL OF SHIT! Riding a bike to nowhere! . . .

ROCK

That is keeping fit! Keeping fit is knowing your shit! You ain't fit. You ain't fitter than shit!

JOHN

Watch this! *(Taking a huge slug.)*

60

ROCK

You have a BIG PROBLEM, pal.

JOHN

YOU got a problem . . . the problem is you . . . and . . .
(points through the door) . . . and HIM . . .

ROCK

Your buddy? He seems pretty cool.

JOHN

He ain't cool at all! He's goin' out with THAT GIRL and I
don't LIKE HER. She gives 'im all these drugs — all the time.
He used to be really smart, Sid . . . But now, he's a BOZO . . .
Fuck!!

ROCK

There's money to be made from acting like a bozo. I've been
there.

Rock touches John's leg, attempting to calm him down. John flinches away.

ROCK

Look, John. Your buddy seems like a real natural. But . . .
people do what they want to do . . . and if that's the way he's
gonna go, there ain't nothing you can do about it. If I was
you, I'd distance myself from him.

Rock's secretary hovers in the doorway with the telephone.

JOHN

Just like that?

SECRETARY

Rock.

ROCK

Yeah . . .

SECRETARY

Long distance . . .

ROCK

(Adjusting his hair) Gotta go . . .

JOHN

My buddy's a natural, all right!! A natural FUCKING JUNKY!!

————— ————— ————— ————— ————— —————

MALCOLM'S OFFICE, INTERIOR, NIGHT

*The upstairs office of the Pistols' Company. Malcolm, Phoebe, John, Paul
and Steve burn the midnight oil. All very serious.*

JOHN

Look. We have to be shot of him and that's that. Right?

PAUL

For Christ's sake, Malcolm. I know WE'RE not great shakes, but the bass player HAS to keep the beat.

STEVE

We have to turn his amp off half the time. He'll be playin' one thing, we'll be playing a fuckin' 'nother.

MALCOLM

Lads. I sympathize. But Sidney's more than a mere bass player. He's a fabulous disaster! He's a symbol! . . . a metaphor! He embodies the dementia of a nihilistic generation! He's a FUCKIN' STAR! He's bigger than any of you.

JOHN

He's a fuckin' headcase.

MALCOLM

Yeah, he's that too. But Sidney's not the problem. The problem, as you're all aware . . .

The phone rings.

PHOEBE

(To telephone) Shut up.

MALCOLM

Phoebe!

She picks it up.

PHOEBE

It's Spunkin. She wants you to book them a suite at —
WHERE? — Rock Head's hotel.

PAUL

Well, fuck that! I want a suite 'n all.

MALCOLM

I would like to suck every live corpuscle from her skinny body and throw the desiccated husk onto the dehydrated shores of Ozymandias!

STEVE

You don't half talk some shit, Malcom.

MALCOLM

Half my charm, sugar.

STEVE

Where the fuck's Ozzy Mandis?

MALCOLM

(Reaching into his drawer for an article) Refers to a pair of feet found in the Gobi Desert. *(Reads)* 'I am Ozymandias, King of Kings, Lord of Lords. Look upon my works ye mighty and despair! Nothing else remains' . . .

STEVE

Oh. Right.

——— ——— ——— ——— ——— ———

HOTEL, SID AND NANCY'S SUITE, INTERIOR, DAY

Sid and Nancy have moved into Rock Head's suite and trashed it.

SID

What do you mean you fucked him? What'd you fuck him for?

NANCY

I fucked him cause he was SEXY, Sid. That's why I fuck guys, usually. Except in CHARITY CASES like yours . . .

SID

I don't want to hear about it! I don't need to know about the PRICKS YOU'VE FUCKED!

NANCY	SID
Fuck you. I've fucked five guys in one night. Chicks, too. I've been paid to fuck, I made a PORNO MOVIE . . .	I've laid eight birds at the same time. I've had fifteen women in the SAME AFTERNOON! Shut up! I fucked a SHEEP!

Sid jumps Nancy, wrestles her on to the bed. She struggles fiercely.

NANCY
Stop! Don't do that!

SID
This dirty film you made — can I see it?

———— ———— ———— ———— ———— ————

HOTEL, EXTERIOR, DAY

Phoebe and Clive emerge from a taxi. Clive wears a trilby hat and shades.

CLIVE
I don't know, Phoebe — he's going to kill me!

PHOEBE
Oh, shut up! It's too late to back out now. Come on!

They enter the hotel.

———— ———— ———— ———— ———— ————

HOTEL CORRIDOR, INTERIOR, DAY

Phoebe and Clive trail after the assistant manager. He wears a butler suit and jangles keys.

ASSISTANT MANAGER
They can't stay here much longer. The police were around
yesterday. ARRESTS were made. SUBSTANCES confiscated.
They've been hanging out of windows.

He taps on their door. No answer. Unlocks it.

———— ———— ———— ———— ———— ————

HOTEL, SID AND NANCY'S SUITE, INTERIOR, DAY

*The suite is empty. One window is open. Outside hangs Nancy, laughing and
screaming, upside down.*

NANCY
All right! I love you! I'm sorry about your goddamn T-shirt!
PULL ME UP! *(Spots Phoebe)* Oh Phoebe! Help! Sid, we've
got company! Let me up!

*Phoebe and Clive, closely followed by the assistant manager rush to the
fire escape.*

HOTEL ROOF, EXTERIOR, DAY

Nancy and Sid stage a mock ambush with their cap guns and then nestle lovey-dovey among the gables.

PHOEBE
Nancy, are you all right?

NANCY
Oh yeah. We're just having fun!

SID
It's Lurch!!

NANCY
You wanna cuppa tea? *(To assistant manager.)* BRING US SOME TEA!

SID
Yeah, four sugars, you cunt!

ASSISTANT MANAGER
Madam, we have no Roof Service.

PHOEBE
We haven't got time for tea, he's got a DENTAL APPOINT-MENT.

SID
Oh, no. I don't wanna go. I wanna stay here and have a really good screw — and go bye-byes!

PHOEBE
Look, if you don't go your teeth are gonna end up like John's.

NANCY
(Pushing him up) Ugghh! SIDNEY, GO!

SID
All right. You comin' wiv me?

CLIVE
I'll go with yer, Sid.

PHOEBE
(Brightly) Anyone for shopping?

NANCY
Shopping?!

PHOEBE
Yeah. You wanna go shopping?

SID
SHOPPING! DENTIST!

STREET, EXTERIOR, DAY

Sid and Clive en route to the dentist. Sid sports a hammer and sickle T-shirt.

CLIVE
Wish I was going to America. Will you still do laundry with us when you come back, Sid?

SID
Oh yeah. Of course. I'm not going to get all starry, you know. I won't let go of my head. I love the laundry . . . it's my second home. I love doin' Nancy's wash. I love folding her knickers.

Wally is walking towards them, wearing a tartan bondage suit. Holding a religious hand-out.

WALLY
Repent! Slack off!

SID
Good God! It's a flying Scotsman!

WALLY
(Turning round to walk with them.) 'The world ends tomorrow and you may die!' . . . Have you seen this? 'The church of the Sub-Genius could save your sanity' . . . this is the man, look, J.R. Bob Dobbs — he's a top man. You should check this out, Clive . . . 'Have intercourse with a beautiful live girl' . . .

SID
(Reading) '. . . state of the church of macho irony . . .'

WALLY
'. . . become physically attractive overnight! . . .'

CLIVE
You know Sid's going to America?

66

WALLY
Yeah, I'm going as well. I'm starting up a religion. Look,
'£20 for membership and ordainment' . . .

CLIVE
Jah Clive! Jah Clive! Jah Clive!

———— ———— ———— ———— ———— ————

KNIGHTSBRIDGE, EXTERIOR, DAY

*Nancy and Phoebe emerge with bulging Harrods bags. Nancy is loud,
exhilarated, up. Phoebe is very edgy.*

NANCY
This place is so NEAT! It's my favourite store in the world
after BLOOMINGDALES! Let's go to KNIGHTSBRIDGE!

PHOEBE
Don't you want to go somewhere a bit more PUNK, Nancy?

NANCY
Not if Malcolm's paying for it!

Nancy piles into the waiting cab. Outside, Phoebe whispers to the driver.

PHOEBE
Heathrow Airport, please.

———— ———— ———— ———— ———— ————

DENTIST'S, INTERIOR, DAY

*Sid sits in the chair. The dentist, a West Indian woman, peruses his pegs.
Wally and Clive look anxiously on.*

DENTIST
When was the last time you had a check up, Mr Richie?

SID
. . . er, 1968. Summer of Love, hur, hur. *(Belches)* Can I
have some GAS?

DENTIST
I'm only LOOKING at your teeth at the moment, Mr
Richie —

SID
Yeah, well. Give me some gas cos it puts me at ease.

CLIVE
Go on. Give him some gas.

WALLY
Can I have some gas, too?

67

DENTIST
Well, all right. *(To Clive)* Do you want some too?

CLIVE
No. No, thanks. I don't do drugs.

SID
You're a fool!

——— ——— ——— ——— ——— ———

TAXI, INTERIOR, DAY

Nancy opens packages, pulls out a big shiny meat cleaver.

NANCY
Oh! you think my Grandpa could use this?

PHOEBE
How long are you staying in England?

NANCY
I'm NEVER going home! . . . WHY?

PHOEBE
Nothing. I just — well, Malcolm and I were talking — we thought you looked a bit PEAKY . . .

NANCY
This isn't Knightsbridge. Where are we going, Phoebe?

PHOEBE
Sort of like you could use a HOLIDAY. . .

NANCY
DRIVER! Where are you going?

DRIVER
Heathrow, innit?

NANCY
HEATHROW! What are you DOING?

PHOEBE
I'm not doing anything.

——— ——— ——— ——— ——— ———

DENTIST'S, INTERIOR, DAY

Sid wakes up with a mouthful of dental tools with Clive and Wally still standing over him.

SID
Nancy?

CLIVE

Give 'im some more gas!

SID

NANCY!

TRAFALGAR SQUARE, EXTERIOR, DAY

Nancy throws herself out of the cab and marches through dangerous traffic, hefting Harrods bags, pursued by Phoebe. Tourists collide. Nancy is hysterical and furious, screaming, eyes glazed.

NANCY

Let me out, you fucking bastards! Bastards! Who's idea was it, anyway — MALCOLM'S! Bastard!

PHOEBE

Nancy!

NANCY

Bastards! Everybody hates me and my Sid!

PHOEBE

We don't hate you, Nancy. It's just I don't think you and Sid bring out the BEST in each other . . .

NANCY

BOLLOCKS! We LOVE each other! Nothing else matters! NOTHING! Wait'll Sid hears about this. He'll tear Malcolm's head off! He'll rip your face off! Cunt! He'll get the MAFIA on you! We have CONNECTIONS! *(Hitting two innocent bystanders with Harrods bags)* Fuck off, you assholes! Leave me fucking alone!

PHOEBE

DO YOU KNOW WHAT'S THE MATTER WITH YOU? YOU'RE A FUCKING HEAD CASE!!!

As Nancy moves off across the Square, Phoebe throws her arms up and storms off in the opposite direction.

KING'S ROAD, EXTERIOR, DAY

A conservatively attired gentleman enters Malcolm's shop walking past two policemen.

———— ———— ———— ———— ———— ————

MALCOLM'S SHOP, INTERIOR, DAY

The gentleman walks up to the counter and whispers.

> GENT
> Do you have any of the SPECIAL STUFF?

> BRENDA
> THE BONDAGE ITEMS! In the back, sir!

> MALCOLM
> The Garden of Eden is straight through there, sir. Don't let the crack of whips put you off!

Brenda lights a match. Malcolm blows it out.

> MALCOLM
> Brenda, my dear. Our future is in your hands! . . . If I'd wanted a tinder box for a shop assistant — I would have advertised for one. Behave yourself! *(Takes box of matches from Brenda.)*

The phone rings.

> MALCOLM
> PHOEBE!!

> BRENDA
> She ain't here.

> MALCOLM
> Brenda!

> BRENDA
> I'm serving a customer!

> MALCOLM
> *(Picks up phone testily)* Yes. What is it? . . .

———— ———— ———— ———— ———— ————

MALCOLM'S SHOP, EXTERIOR, DAY

Sid slams along the street, knocks over two policemen and dives into the shop.

MALCOLM'S SHOP, INTERIOR, DAY

Sid storms in. Malcolm is gone.

> SID
> ALL RIGHT! Where is he? WHERE IS HE?

> BRENDA
> Who?

Sid grabs hold of several customers and hurls them out of the door.

> SID
> Fuck off! Get out of here, you cunts! . . . MALCOLM!!
> *(Grabbing the gent.)* And you, you cunt. GET OUT!!

Sid starts knocking the shop up and pulling clothes off rails.

> SID
> Where is he? MALCOLM! Fucking where is he?

> BRENDA
> He hasn't been in today.

> SID
> LUCKY FOR HIM! If he was here now, he'd be fucking
> DEAD. I'd fucking tear his eyes out! Anybody wants to fuck
> with Nancy GOT TO FUCK WITH ME FIRST!!

Sid rages up and down. Falls exhausted on the floor. Incoherent.

> You know he was going to put her on a plane — you know,
> I can't even ENTERTAIN the idea! . . . without her
> Methadone . . . you know it's really FUCKING STUPID!
> What if she died? He'd be a MURDERER! I'LL FUCKING
> KILL HIM! She's all I got — I'm in love with her . . . WE'RE
> ONE.

Sid wipes his eyes. Brenda, crying too, gets down on the floor and puts her arm round him.

> I'm sorry about all this . . . I've made a right mess of your
> shelves . . .

> BRENDA
> I'm sorry. I had no idea.

> SID
> You got a cigarette? . . .

> BRENDA
> Yeah.

Brenda reaches for a match in her pocket. Can't find one. Malcolm, hiding under the counter, has just lit up.

BRENDA
Shit! I ain't got a light!

—————— —————— —————— —————— —————— ——————

EGG 'N' CHIPS CAFE, INTERIOR, NIGHT

Phoebe, Malcolm, John, Steve, Paul, Sid and Nancy. Very tense. Everyone except Phoebe wears shades.

MALCOLM
All right. Four words. No Women On The Tour.

PHOEBE
That's five words.

NANCY
NO WAY, MALCOLM. No fuckin' way!

SID
Yeah, right. There's no way.

PHOEBE
Look, it's purely financial. We can't AFFORD a — an entourage —

NANCY
I'M NOT AN ENTOURAGE!

PHOEBE
— on the tour. Look, I know what you're feeling. I KNOW how important your relationship is. If you two want to stay together, we'll JUST HAVE to find ANOTHER BASS PLAYER.

NANCY
Sid Vicious IS the Sex Pistols.

STEVE
Bollocks!

SID
No, that's right. You can't leave me behind. Paul wouldn't stand for it. We're the rhythm section. Right, Paul?

Paul does not respond.

PHOEBE
Look, it's only a month. You can live that long without each other, can't you?

Sid puts his arm around Nancy. He does not reply.

MALCOLM
If you DO survive — I have been talking to the record

company and they're going to buy you a little house!

JOHN
Aaahh — how lovely for you!

NANCY
(Crying) You think I'm an asshole, don't you?

JOHN
Yes. I do.

NANCY
You really think that you can BUY Sid off me. Well fuck you. Take him. I only want what's best for Sidney. I don't want to go on your fucking tour anyhow . . . I've got my OWN STUFF to do . . .

SID
Paul. Paul.

———— ———— ———— ———— ———— ————

HOTEL BEDROOM, INTERIOR, NIGHT

Nancy and Sid finish fucking. Sid lays his head on the pillow.

NANCY
Sid.

SID
What are you doing . . .?

NANCY
Sid. Stay awake.

SID
No. I'm tired. I gotta get up in a couple of hours.

NANCY
I know. . . these are our last two hours together. Stay awake.

SID
What for?

NANCY
So I can talk to you. So we can fuck some more. So we can be together.

SID
We ARE together. C'mon, gimme a break — ay?

NANCY
NO. You give ME a break. I'm the one that's getting left behind. Kiss my toes.

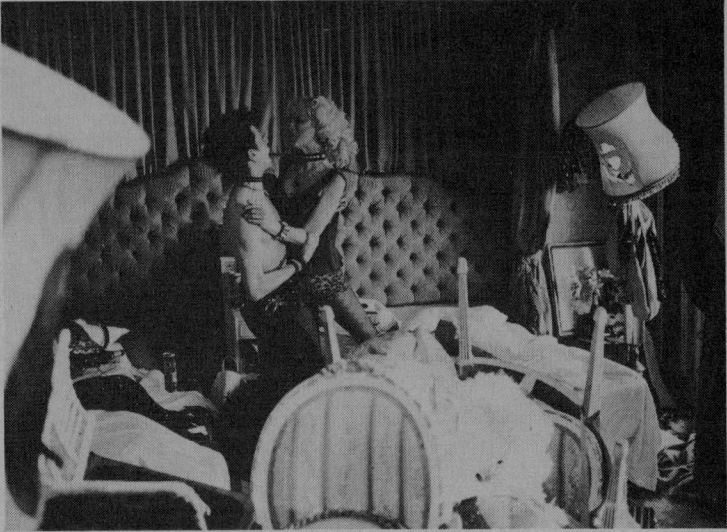

SID
(Turning over) Oh, fuck off!

NANCY
(Clouting him) Fuck YOU!

Sid jumps out of bed; starts pulling on his pants and leather jacket.

SID
Fuck this! Jesus!

NANCY
Where are you going? Where are you going? Stop it, SID!
Come back!

SID
I'm going to the airport. Gonna be early for once. You know
what I mean?

NANCY
WHAT ARE YOU DOING?! Sid! Sid, don't be a jerk. Fuck it,
Sid. Don't leave! SID!!! What about the FAREWELL
DRUGS?

*Sid slams out. Nancy, tearful, pulls out the drugs. Faces the wall with
eyedropper and needle, scratching for a vein.*

NANCY
(Softly) Come back, Sid. Don't be a jerk . . .

74

TWO LANE BLACKTOP, EXTERIOR, DAY

The Sex Pistols Tour Bus rolls towards us. Covered in graffiti, preceded by the Shovel Heads Motorcycle Club, pursued by two huge peterbilts, buzzed by a helicopter.

TOUR BUS, INTERIOR, DAY

John and Sid sit at opposing windows near the front of the bus. Paul and Steve sit at the back, surrounded by passed-out roadies. John watches Sid's laborious attempts to write postcards. Sid keeps getting stuck and screwing them up. John hacks and sniffles from a severe cold.

> JOHN
> Lacking in communication skills?

> SID
> Fuck off! I'm an ace communicator. Oy! Me and Steve was talking to some kids after the show. Oy, Steve! STEVE! They said that you were really stuck up and that you don't talk to anybody.

> JOHN
> Yeah, well. Neither do you. You just sit there smacked out and drooling.

> SID
> Yeah, well, I've still got ten times more charisma than you. Malcolm said so!

> JOHN
> Bollocks. Malcolm never said that. Did he?

> SID
> Oy! How d'ya spell holiday?

> JOHN
> S.H.I.T.

> SID
> *(Writing)* Dear Mum, having a lovely . . .
> You cunt!!!

GREAT SOUTHEAST MUSIC HALL, ATLANTA, EXTERIOR, NIGHT

Located in a shopping mall, the show is oversold. A huge crowd of kids, reporters, vice cops and sociologists cheer, whistle and applaud outside.

MUSIC HALL, STAGE, INTERIOR, NIGHT

The Pistols perform 'Holidays In The Sun'. A punkette nuts Sid as he plays.

>JOHN
>*(Mid-song)* Aren't we the worst thing you've ever seen?

Sid smears the blood over his face and torso.

——— ——— ——— ——— ——— ———

FRIED CHICKEN, INTERIOR, DUSK

Steve and Paul sit with some local cowboys. They are very depressed.

——— ——— ——— ——— ——— ———

FRIED CHICKEN, EXTERIOR, DUSK

Sid is outside on the phone, swigging from a bottle.

>SID
>Yeah, Nancy! . . . yeah well — Mrs Spungen . . . BEVERLY!
>Look under Beverly. No? Well, Spungen. Mrs Spungen!
>. . . What! No Spungen! . . . What do you mean? . . . WHAT?
>. . . FUCK IT!! *(Slams the phone down)* Fucking poxy place!

——— ——— ——— ——— ——— ———

TOUR BUS, INTERIOR, DAY

The bus is passing through poverty and desolation. Sid pours vodka end-lessly into his mouth. John sitting next to a record exec. looks on with disdain.

Sid's Shovel Head minder walks down the aisle to sit next to Sid. The minder takes the bottle from him and folds his arms, then unfolds them and folds Sid's arms too.

76

EXECUTIVE
Ah, it's a great tour, John. GREAT tour, GREAT country!

JOHN
Ah, it's lovely! It's a pity it's America.

EXECUTIVE
Right! Did you know that I was a bit of a songster myself?
Bet you didn't know that, did you?

JOHN
Ah, I didn't . . .

EXECUTIVE
It's true! I've written a lot of songs! Speaking of unemploy-
ment, I've written one lately — that you might like because
it has a — PUNKY — punky sort of feel — know what I
mean?

JOHN
Oh, how INTERESTING . . .

EXECUTIVE
Really! It's called 'I want a job'. *(Singing)*
I want a job
I want a job
I want a good job
I want a job that pays
I want a job
I want a job
I want a good job
One that satisfies
My artistic
Needs.
(Stops singing) That's just the chorus!

JOHN
Oh. What's it called again?

EXECUTIVE
It's called 'I Want A Job'.

JOHN
Oh, lovely . . .

EXECUTIVE
Do you think you boys might have any interest in that one?

JOHN
Here, Sid! SID! You heard this?

SID
What . . .

EXECUTIVE
Oh no, don't embarrass me, please.

JOHN
No, go on . . .

He sings it again. Raucous laughter from Sid.

EXECUTIVE
You like it, Sid?

JOHN
Stupid cunt!!

EXECUTIVE
(To John) Sid?

————— ————— ————— ————— —————

ON STAGE, INTERIOR, NIGHT

The Pistols perform 'Pretty Vacant'. A drunk cowboy hangs onto John's leg. Sid whacks him with his guitar and gets carried off by the crowd.

————— ————— ————— ————— —————

RAILWAY TRACKS, EXTERIOR, LATER

'Pretty Vacant' continues. Outside Shovel Heads wearing 'Sex Pistols Security' badges, bounce Sid around.

Malcolm and Sid's minder come to the rescue.

SID'S MINDER
He can't fight for shit!

MALCOLM
He likes it!

————— ————— ————— ————— —————

SUNSHINE INN, EXTERIOR, NIGHT

The motel forecourt is in ruins. While the minder carries the unconscious Sid Malcolm starts spraying further insults on the tour bus.

MALCOLM
Our Sid is not vicious. That's just our pet name for him. He's named after a hamster . . . what is a hamster, I hear you ask . . . A hamster is a very talented, but highly unpredictable little gerbil. At the moment, our little animal is a very sick bloke. Look after him, will you? He needs it! Make sure he doesn't get too WASTED . . .

SUNSHINE INN ROOM, INTERIOR, NIGHT

Sid is in a room packed with proto-punks, teenage Texas belles in spandex and leopard skin. Sex Pistols tapes playing loud.

Surrounded by most of them, Sid is lying on the bed, carving 'Nancy' on his chest, with a razor.

> LINDA
> He's BESOTTED with you, Nancy. I don't know how you stand it.

> NANCY
> Because I love him . . .

———— ———— ———— ———— ———— ————

BUCKINGHAM PALACE, EXTERIOR, DAY

Nancy and Linda sitting with a bottle in a bag. Strung out.

> NANCY
> It's probably over already and I don't know it . . .

> LINDA
> Now don't start feeling fucking sorry for yourself. You're not dead yet!

> NANCY
> Yeah . . . but I'm gonna be and it's gonna be great!
> Think the Queen's home?

> LINDA
> Nah . . . They put a flag out.

> NANCY
> Well, there's a light on. Who's that?

> LINDA
> Mrs Thatcher trying out the beds.

> NANCY
> Who's that?

———— ———— ———— ———— ———— ————

LINDA'S PAD, INTERIOR, DAY

Nancy answers the phone. She wears dominatrix gear.

> NANCY
> Hello? SID! Where are you? I thought you'd hate me for ever. I was going crazy for you. I miss you too. How do you

like America? I never want to fight with you again. And you
left all that money. I love you. I split it with Linda. Did you
buy me any PRESENTS yet?

LINDA

Nancy.

NANCY

I wish I was there too, Sid. I really do. I love you. Look I
can't talk right now. Linda's got a customer.

Sid goes on talking. Linda calls again. Nancy gets antsy.

Sidney, I've got to go. We're working. I wish we could too.
But I'm in England and you're in America . . .

LINDA

NANCY!

NANCY

I'm sorry, Sid, but we can't. You'll just have to have sex with
someone else!

*Nancy hangs up the phone. She's upset. Takes several deep breaths, rubs at
the corner of her eyes, stalks into the adjacent room.*

LINDA'S PAD, ADJACENT ROOM, INTERIOR, DAY

Another rich masochist hangs from the wall. Linda hands Nancy a whip.

LINDA

You've been a naughty, naughty newsreader. Now you're
gonna PAY.

*She and Nancy take alternate swipes at his hairy white back. Linda's swipes
are light and delicate. Nancy flogs him viciously.*

LINDA

(Whispering) Not so hard. Not so HARD. NANCY!

TWO LANE BLACKTOP, EXTERIOR, DAY

*Another one of those piled-up telephoto shots with lots of American stuff in
it.*

PAUL

(Voice over) How come we can't fly in the plane with
Malcolm?

PHOEBE

(Voice over) Because the bus is more fun.

TOUR BUS, INTERIOR, DAY

Sid accosts Steve and his latest girlfriends.

> SID
> Oy, Stevey baby, I've shagged more women than you've had
> hot dinners! I'm a better fighter too! Go on, fuckin' hit me!

> STEVE
> Oh, sit down, will yer — stop yer noise.

> PHOEBE
> Shut up, Sidney. Why are you being such a wind-up?

Sid lurches down the aisle of the bus and half straddles Phoebe in her seat.

> SID
> I don't know. Sex-t-ual tension I suppose . . . 'ere c'mon
> Phoebs . . . give us a portion!

> PHOEBE
> Oh look, why pick on me! There must be thousands of
> women out there that want to fuck Sid Vicious!

> SID
> Really?

——— ——— ——— ——— ——— ———

ON STAGE, INTERIOR, NIGHT

The Pistols at the end of a song. Sid moves to the front of the stage.

> SID
> Right! Who's gonna fuck me then?

Teenage Texan girls and punkettes reach out for him.

MEXICAN BAR, DALLAS, INTERIOR, NIGHT

Sid is attached to an electric shock machine. He is surrounded by a pack of admiring manly men. John walks in through the saloon doors of the bar.

    JOHN
Hey! Amigo! Can I have a Sea Breeze, please!

    SID
What a stupid fuckin' hat you're wearing — you got some FLARED TROUSERS to go with it?

    JOHN
I cannot begin to understand the SHALLOWNESS of your INTELLECT, Sidney.

The manly men become admiring transvestites as Sid is preparing for a higher voltage.

    SID
Go on! Give it some more you wally!

    JOHN
If you weren't such a slave to your libido, you might realise what's happened to your BRAIN!

    SID
Aaagh! Aaagh! Fuck! Aahh . . . *(His eyes roll back. He collapses to the floor.)*

LINDA'S PAD, INTERIOR, DAY

Nancy and Linda at the breakfast table wearing Linda's kimonos. Linda smokes a lot. The phone rings. Nancy picks it up.

    NANCY
Hello?

    SID
Hello! Hello, it's me!

NANCY
SID!

SID
How you doing?

NANCY
What? Where are you? What are you doing?

SID
I'm fucking a TV.

NANCY
You're what? Fucking a television?

SID
Nah. You know. A bloke with a wig on!

NANCY
Linda. Sid's doing it with a TRANSVESTITE. *(Into phone)*
Is she a TV or a SEX CHANGE?

SID
What?

NANCY
Does she have a cock?

SID
I don't know.

——— ——— ——— ——— ——— ———

SUNSHINE INN, BEDROOM, INTERIOR, NIGHT

*Sid lies in bed with a suspicious blonde on top of him talking to Nancy on
the phone.*

NANCY
Well, go on. Look!

SID
Yeah. Shit! Does that mean he's a bloke? I love you . . .

——— ——— ——— ——— ——— ———

LINDA'S PAD, INTERIOR, DAY

NANCY
Have you touched her cock yet, Sid? Well go on. Touch it.
Pretend she's you and you're me. *(Lights up another cigarette
and listens. To Linda)* Is this perverted? Do you think I'm
WEIRD?

Fade up sounds of Winterland.

SID'S VOICE
(Amplified) Whoever hit me on the head, it didn't hurt a
bit!

———— ———— ———— ———— ———— ————

AUDITORIUM, SAN FRANCISCO, INTERIOR, NIGHT

*The Sex Pistols' last gig. The band all hate each other. Everybody yells at
everybody else, backstage and front. Sid plays bass with only one string.
A Peruvian film crew sits astride the shoulders of armed bodyguards.*

STEVE
Is this Johnny Rotten?

SID
Nah. I've only used it twice!

JOHN
(Off mike) Oh yes, yes. Very funny. The naive wit of
imbeciles has always enchanted me.

SID
Why don't you shut up and fucking sing, you twat!

PAUL
You're well out of time, Sid.

SID
Bollocks! You wanker!

STEVE
Fucking play the song, will ya.

JOHN
(Over mike) Ever get the feeling you're being CHEATED?
. . . 1. 2. 3. 4. . . .

They launch into 'Problems'. Malcolm and Phoebe watch anxiously from the side of the stage.

——— ——— ——— ——— ——— ———

LIMO, INTERIOR, NIGHT

John and Sid sit in opposite corners, not talking. The limo pulls up outside the hotel ballroom. Sid starts to get out. John stays put.

SID
(Reading) 'Welcome Sex Pistols'. Fools! Coming to the party then?

JOHN
Nah . . . I don't think so . . . I don't feel too good . . . Maybe later.

SID
Fucking typical.

Sid slams the door. John heaves a racking cough and spits blood into his hand.

Sid walks towards the reception doors and is greeted by a group of Shovel Heads leaving the party.

SHOVEL HEADS
Hey, Sid! All right!

He turns to salute and then reverses straight through the plateglass door.

——— ——— ——— ——— ——— ———

HOTEL BALLROOM, INTERIOR, NIGHT

Sid rolls in the broken glass, spilling blood. The crowded reception is brought to a standstill. Sid tries to rise, falls down again.

——— ——— ——— ——— ——— ———

HOTEL, EXTERIOR, NIGHT

John stares from the passenger window of the limo.

JOHN
Typical.

Sid is being treated by a doctor. He is almost all bandages. Malcolm, Phoebe, John, Paul, Steve and a tanned and sultry blonde in attendance. Only the blonde does not notice the tension in the air.

>   BLONDE
> How fascinating to be meeting Ronnie Biggs and Rio is so lovely at this time of year. Will you be staying for Carnival?
>
>   JOHN
> Tell that fucking woman to SHUT UP!
>
>   STEVE
> Tell 'er yourself, ya twerp!
>
>   JOHN
> No. You tell her. I am not a fucking twerp.
>
>   PHOEBE
> SHUT THE FUCK UP! *(They do.)* It's about time somebody came out in the open.
>
>   PAUL
> I want to leave the band. *(Gets up and leaves the room.)*
>
>   STEVE
> Yeah. I do as well.
>
>   JOHN
> Oh, fine! Fine! The sidemen split. GOODBYE! *(Steve gets up.)* Yeah, well, why don't you take 'im with you! Cunts! You're not leaving me with USELESS are you?
>
>   STEVE
> He's your friend, John.
>
>   JOHN
> OH, NO THANK YOU, STEVIE!
>
>   STEVE
> Oh, fuck off!
>
>   JOHN
> NO! YOU FUCK OFF!
>
>   MALCOLM
> I'm bored.

Malcolm leaves. The doctor shakes a bottle of pills at Sid. No response. He leaves them anyway.

HAIGHT ASHBURY, EXTERIOR, DAY

Phoebe emerges from Uganda liquors with an armful of comic books and candy. She gets into the waiting taxi cab.

――――― ――――― ――――― ――――― ――――― ―――――

TAXI CAB, INTERIOR, DAY

Sid grabs the comic books and chocolates.

> SID
> I wish we wasn't breaking up.

> PHOEBE
> Well, it's a bit late for that innit? Malcolm's in London. Paul and Steve are flying to Rio. John's in New York.

> SID
> Oh, great. What am I going to do?

> PHOEBE
> Anything you like. You're a free agent now.

> SID
> I wanna go home . . . see Nancy.

> PHOEBE
> Yeah. Well, do that – and look, while you're there, do me a favour? Go on a programme. Get off the heroin.

> SID
> Oh, come on. I can't think about myself at the moment. I've got to think about her. She's got a lot of problems . . .
> *(Indicates comic)* Master of Kung Fu!

> PHOEBE
> Look – you might help her with her problems if you both got straight.

> SID
> Do us a favour! You don't understand, do you? I love her. She needs me. I'll do anything she wants me to . . .

> PHOEBE
> Oh, yeah – that includes killing yourself as well, does it?

> SID
> *(Shrugs)* Oh, bollocks! Now you're talking like a grown up. I hate grown ups. They got no intelligence whatsoever. In any case, I'll be dead by the time I'm 24 . . .

> PHOEBE
> Look, who the bloody hell do you think you're talking to, a

REPORTER? Look, I've known you since you were 13 and if you love Nancy, you'd be looking out for her. For Christ's sake! You're only 20. You're too smart to be so bloody stupid. Look, just try and get off the heroin then, ey?

                    SID
Yeah, all right . . .

                    PHOEBE
Come on, promise.

                    SID
All right.

                    PHOEBE
And the pills. No more pills!

                    SID
Okay.

                    PHOEBE
And cut down on the drinking.

                    SID
Yeah. All right. I promise.

———— ———— ———— ———— ———— ————

BOEING 747, INTERIOR, DAY

Sid sits on an aisle seat reading his comic books. A steward approaches with his beverage.

                    STEWARD
Your double brandy, sir.

Sid takes it, pulls out a handful of Valiums, washes them down.

———— ———— ———— ———— ———— ————

AIRPORT, EXTERIOR, DUSK

The 747 lands against a backdrop of stormclouds.

                    RADIO VOICE
Sex Pistol Sid Vicious landed in New York this afternoon. Vicious was carried off a plane and taken to a hospital in Queens. A spokesman for the record company said Vicious was suffering from NERVOUS EXHAUSTION . . .

HOSPITAL, EXTERIOR, NIGHT

It is snowing.

> SID'S VOICE
>
> *(On radio)* Yeah, well what happened was I done the rest of my junk and some sulphate and about six or seven downers. And when you get high in the air you get much higher than you do on the ground . . .

> RADIO VOICE
>
> Exclusive interview with **SID VICIOUS** coming up on this station at **NINE O' CLOCK.**

——— ——— ——— ——— ——— ———

HOSPITAL ROOM, INTERIOR, NIGHT

Sid lays in bed attached to an IV. Plateglass snowy Manhattan night outside.

The door opens.

A squeaking shopping cart rolls in. It's loaded with gaily wrapped presents, Candyland game, chocs, Marvel comics, a dead Xmas tree. Sid stares at it.

Nancy follows it in.

——— ——— ——— ——— ——— ———

PARIS, FRANCE, MONTAGE

Sid and Nancy visit Paris in the spring. They go shopping, eat pastries, beat up a hippie busker in the Metro, nod out at a café on the Champs Elysées and are refused admittance to the Lido — a big shouting match ensues.

SID	NANCY
Dear Mum,	Dear Mom,
Guess where your Simon has turned up? Since you can't guess I will tell you. Paris. Paris is all right. I enclose some money so you can get the phone put back. Please stop giving interviews. Your loving Simon. P.S. Nancy sends her love.	Guess where we both are? Paris. In the spring. Sid is recording here and is just brilliant. We go shopping every day. Sid has bought me lots of underwear and it is all French. Pierre Clementi. You would love it here. Lots of love from Nancy and Sid. XXX

CAFE OUTSIDE THE MOULIN ROUGE, EXTERIOR, NIGHT

Sid and Nancy sit at a café table searching their pockets for money. The waiter arrives and puts the bill on their table.

> NANCY
>
> Yeah. Ah, great! Great, yeah — thanks! GREAT? Sid, what have we got to pay for this. You lost it.

> SID
>
> *(Searching pockets)* No. No I lost it —

Hugh Kares spots Sid. Hugh wears designer bell bottoms and rose-tinted shades. He guides his designer anorexic wife to a halt beside their table.

> HUGH
>
> Sidney!! Long time no see. Hugh Kares. We met at Trumps! You remember!

> NANCY
>
> No, he doesn't. Sid!

> SID
>
> This is my girlfriend, Nancy.

> HUGH
>
> Hi, Nancy. So, Sidney, who's handling you management-wise.

> NANCY
>
> Piss off! Sid!

> HUGH
>
> Sidney. Let's get together. Let's take lunch.

Hugh's anorexic wife looks angry and hits him on the shoulder.

> Will you just get yourself a chair and sit down. Shut up! *(Turning back to Sid)*. We'll go to La Coupole — we'll eat foods that we can't even name. Sidney, me and you. We'll sit together. Everything's crazy for me right now but, Sid, I always got time for you, babe. I love ya! I love ya!

Sid suddenly doubles up and vomits over Hugh.

> HUGH
>
> Jesus Christ! That's all right! That's all right . . . get it all out, Sidney.

> NANCY
>
> He feels fine. It's you who's making him sick. Sid, let's go.

> HUGH
>
> When you're feeling better, Sid. When you're feeling better . . .

Sid still coughing, points at Hugh's anorexic wife.

          NANCY
Why are you wearing that thing?

          HUGH'S WIFE
(Jaw wired shut) **I'g og a dieg.**

          NANCY
Yeah. It's not working.

Nancy hustles Sid away.

          HUGH
You're going to make somebody a lot of money, Sidney!!

———— ———— ———— ———— ———— ————

THEATRE, INTERIOR, DAY

Sid stands at the top of a flight of neon steps. He squints into the lights. Video monitors glow.

The opening strains of 'My Way' are heard. Sid lopes down the glowing steps. He wears a white tux, black pants, one of Nancy's garters. Mimes to his recorded voice. Malcolm chatters to Phoebe in the background.

The audience is entranced. At the end of the number, Sid pulls out his magnum and blows the audience away.

Screams, blood packs explode on bejewelled dowagers, old colonels, infatuated débutantes. Sid aims the gun at Malcolm and Phoebe. Packs burst on them as well. He points the gun at Nancy. She nods. Bam. Bam. Bam.

Sid tosses the gun away. He flips 'em off and lopes back up the neon stairs.

Covered in stage blood, Nancy comes back to life. She meets him on the stairs. They kiss. The neons flicker out.

94

MAIDA VALE FLAT, INTERIOR, DAY

Black walls with Sex Pistols posters. Overflowing ashtrays, empty milk bottles, half-consumed food. Black sheets on bed. Nancy is on the phone.

NANCY
(Into phone) It's Nancy. Did Malcolm . . . well, I know he's there . . . well, did he get us that gig

SID
— at the Nashville —

NANCY
— at the Nashville? . . . No, you said that yesterday and you never phoned us back . . . yeah! . . . Well make sure he does! *(Hangs up)* Shit! Fuck Malcolm! I could manage your career better than Malcolm.

SID
Well, why don't you then?

NANCY
I'm NOT Malcolm. I'm a joke . . . Mrs Sid Vicious . . .

SID
Oh, fuck Sid Vicious. Sid Vicious is an ex-Sex Pistol. What's he done lately? . . . I wouldn't be shit without you — you're the only real woman on the planet. Honest, you — you could be my manager. Easy — easy.

NANCY
You mean it?

SID
Yeah. Malcolm McLaren! He couldn't run a fucking bath . . . yeah . . .

NANCY
(In unison with Sid) Oh you **PATHETIC** — **LYING** — **SOD!** *(Fires the toy pistol round her neck).*

———— ———— ———— ———— ———— ————

ALBION ROAD FLAT, INTERIOR, AFTERNOON

Two bearded junkies sit on the floor watching Blue Peter. No furniture. Sid stands at the window flexing his arm. Nancy is shooting up.

SID
All the houses had people in 'em . . . like, a year ago, shops empty shops . . . what happened to that little house . . .?

JUNKY
We chopped it up for firewood.

97

Sid continues to stare out of the window. Outside the leaves rise, gradually, and reattach themselves to trees. Suffused with a golden glow . . . Fade in 'The White Cliffs of Dover'.

JUBILEE STREET PARTY, EXTERIOR, DAY

Bunting, Union Jacks, TV sets in windows, trestle tables in the street. Nazi Skins and Teds mingle with the patriotic old. Kids are stuffed with food. Like VE day. Nancy, Sid and Brenda sit isolated at the end of a trestle table. Nancy and Sid are totally wasted.

> NANCY
> Where's Linda? I haven't seen her for ever —
>
> BRENDA
> Linda?
>
> NANCY
> Yeah, where is she? Is she sick of something?
>
> BRENDA
> She's dead.
>
> NANCY
> Whaa . . .
>
> BRENDA
> It happened really quick, you know. She'd been ill for months and they . . . they diagnosed it as cancer and two weeks later she was dead.
>
> NANCY
> *(In tears)* Oh . . .

Sid puts his arm around her.

> We should have gone to see her. But we never do anything. We just sit around that stupid flat.
>
> BRENDA
> Apparently she left a load of money as well. You know, 'cos she'd been saving up and everything. She left something like ten thousand pounds but she didn't leave no will so the fucking government gets it all.
>
> NANCY
> That sucks . . . she worked really hard for all that . . .
>
> SID
> That's typical . . . you know, if you work and you get any money — and you die — in this country the government gets the whole thing — it's just crap — it doesn't mean a thing —

that's why we're going away . . . to America . . .

SreBRENDA

Oh, what, so you can die rich?

SID

Nah. Nancy's gonna do some modellin' an' get me some gigs. You know, get working again. Get into it.

BRENDA

You don't want to go to America, Sid! You're English. You oughta stay here.

A bunch of skinheads push their way through the crowd and spot Sid, Nancy and Brenda moping. They approach.

SKIN 1
OI! FUCK OFF!!!

SKIN 2
'Ere, Dennis! 'E told you to fuck off!

SKIN 1
You what! You fucking want trouble, cunt?!

The skinheads move in to attack.

CHELSEA HOTEL, INTERIOR, DAY

Sid and Nancy lie side by side in bed in the dark.

NANCY
Seems like all my friends are dead. When I die will you be sad?

SID
I couldn't live without you.

NANCY
You couldn't? We better die together then.

SID
How will we do it?

NANCY
Throw ourselves under a subway. Jump off a building. OD. If I asked you to kill me, would you?

SID
What would I do? I couldn't live without you.

NANCY
You'd kill yourself too, then? Shit. I hate this fuckin' life . . .

SID
Oh, come on. This is just a bad patch. Honest. Look, things will be much better when we get to America. I promise.

NANCY
WE'RE IN AMERICA.

SID
What?

NANCY
We've been here a week. New York is IN America.

SID
Oh, gettaway . . . are we? . . . we're not, gettaway. Are we? *(Struggles out of bed. Starts walking around the room.)*

NANCY
Yeah. What day is it? Shit! Is it Tuesday or Wednesday? We're supposed to be at Granma and Grandpa's on Wednesday . . . where's my fucking book? . . . Shit!

Sid hesitates before going to the window, then pulls back the shutters and pushes the window open.

━━━━━━ ━━━━━━ ━━━━━━ ━━━━━━ ━━━━━━ ━━━━━━

TWENTY-THIRD STREET, NEW YORK, EXTERIOR, DAY

Sid steps on to the balcony of the Chelsea Hotel. They're on the second floor. He is amazed.

━━━━━━ ━━━━━━ ━━━━━━ ━━━━━━ ━━━━━━ ━━━━━━

STATION WAGON, INTERIOR, DAY

Grandpa drives at 15 mph. Cursed by passing drivers. Nancy gives a running commentary on the neighbourhood. Granma outlines the itinerary. Sid swigs schnapps and nods.

GRANMA

Bette, Andy and the kids are coming by at 6.30. Remember
them? They used to be our neightbours. We're eating at 7.15.

NANCY

Nah. I don't want to see them. Nah, they're a drag. We came
to see YOU GUYS.

GRANMA

They want to see YOU, Nancy. They're family too and it's
ALL SET.

NANCY

Fuck it being ALL SET! I hate them. Sid doesn't want to see
them, do you Sidney?

SID

(In Nancy's ear) Look how wide the streets are. Are we on
the freeway?

GRANDPA

Freeway, schmeeway. You like it or you don't like it. This is
how I always drive — for safety.

Grandpa runs another driver off the road.

NANCY

Oh! Oh! Hahahaha . . . Look, there's the ROLLERAMA!
SID! I won a roller skating trophy there when I was six years
old!

GRANMA

Nancy, don't fib.

NANCY

Fuck you, Granma . . . Oh! Oh! It's White Castle! Hahaha!

SID

This place is a fuckin' paradise . . .

—————— —————— —————— —————— —————— ——————

DINING ROOM, INTERIOR, NIGHT

*Sid, Nancy, Andy, Bette and their children, Chipper (17), Buzz (16), and
Mary Jane (13). Granma and Granpa.*

*Deadly silence. All watch as Nancy cuts Sid's food. Nancy drinks vodka tonic,
Sid peppermint schnapps. Everybody else drinks Coke, Tab and Mr Pibb.*

NANCY

You guys got to come and see us in New York when I get Sid
his gigs. Got to.

BUZZ

(Whispering) Hey, Chip. Can't he cut his own meat?

CHIPPER

Shhhh!

NANCY

They really want him at Max's but they're too fucking cheap. They only want to pay him THREE GRAND — I mean he's worth FIVE at least. Sid's a really BIG STAR in New York.

SID

We both are.

NANCY

Yeah, I mean, we hardly have any time to ourselves. It's like, we barely have time to get to the METHADONE CLINIC. We only got enough for two days. You all done? *(Pushes Sid's plate away).* Mary Jane, listen, you wanna come out partying with us? Mmmm. Granma! Can I borrow the car? I wanna teach Sid how to drive American!

CHIPPER

MOM! How come Nancy gets to borrow Granma's car and I don't? She's the one that got FUCKED UP and wrecked it . . .

BETTE

CHIPPER!

NANCY

What do you know, CRATER FACE? Fuckin' twerp. Too bad about your brothers, Mary Jane. Still taking IDIOT LESSONS?

The silence is broken by Granpa's tuneless humming.

GRANPA

So. Are you going to make an honest woman out of our
Nancy, Sid?

SID

Well, she's always been honest to me, Granpa, sir. She's
never lied to me.

GRANPA

But what are your — er — intentions?

SID

Well, first off, we're gonna go down the methadone clinic on
Monday, then Nancy's gonna get me some gigs and then
we're gonna go off and, like, live in Paris. And then just, sort
of, go out in a **BLAZE OF GLORY**. But don't worry. You'll
be proud of us.

GRANPA

So! Why don't we go down to the REC. ROOM!

——————— ——————— ——————— ——————— ——————— ———————

REC. ROOM, INTERIOR, NIGHT

*Pool table. Wet bar. Jukebox. Mini-trampoline. Chipper and Buzz play 'Pong'
at the advent screen. Granma, Granpa, Andy and Bette whisper by the door.
'Bodies' plays on the cassette. Sid attempts to strum the bass line on an old
acoustic guitar.Chipper and Buzz make faces.*

In unison Sid and Nancy sing the chorus from 'Bodies'.

NANCY

(In unison with Sid) **I DON'T WANT A BABY THAT
LOOKS LIKE CHIPPER . . .**

SID

All right, Chipper!

Sid sits down and nods. Mary Jane applauds ecstatically.

NANCY

What else are we going to do?

SID

I'm tired. I want to go noddy blinkums.

NANCY

Oh, OK. Where are we sleeping?

GRANMA

Well, actually dear you're not staying here. We thought it
would be more, um, FUN for you to stay downtown. At the
SUNSHINE INN . . .

NANCY

NO!! What about French toast and blintzes?

GRANMA

No!! You don't WANT to come back HERE for breakfast. Your bus leaves at 9.17.

NANCY

But we're staying another day . . .

GRANMA

Well, Granpa and I must have misunderstood. See, we're – eh – going out of town tomorrow. The whole family is going out of town.

CHIPPER

I didn't know we were going anywhere.

FAMILY

Chipper! Shut up! Be quiet, Chipper!

NANCY

That's all right! Can we come?

GRANMA

NO, Nancy. You just can't.

NANCY

Well, will you at least drive us to the motel?

GRANMA

Of course we will.

GRANPA

We'll give you money for a taxi for tomorrow morning to get you to the bus in plenty of time. LOVELY seeing you, sweetheart darling . . .

Granpa pushes Nancy into her coat. Granma wonders what to do with Sid.

———— ———— ———— ———— ———— ————

SUNSHINE INN ROOM, INTERIOR, NIGHT

TV on. Sid and Nancy in bed. Nancy morose. Sid is attempting to roll a joint.

SID

Those people were really lovely. That house. Pool table – and a bar. It was great! Best fuckin' food I ever ate. So why did they throw us out?

NANCY

'Cause they know me.

104

SID
I really love you.

NANCY
Can you move your foot?

———— ———— ———— ———— ———— ————

METHADONE CLINIC, INTERIOR, DAY

Sid and Nancy stand at the counter filling in the forms while the caseworker scrutinizes them closely.

CASEWORKER
(Measuring out their methadone) You know about the Golden Triangle? That's where the heroin comes from. Heard about it when I was in the Nam. You heard of Vietnam, right?

NANCY
Yup.

CASEWORKER
Yeah. Ahh ah, yeah, while us guys was fighting and getting all fucked up, the CIA was flying the shit out of there and into here, with OUR planes. Know who paid for that shit? WE DID. That is, the government. You know why? Cause smack's the GREAT CONTROLLER. Keeps the people stupid when they could be smart.

SID
What's he on about?

NANCY
Some bullshit politics.

CASEWORKER
You guys got no right to be strung out on this stuff. You could be sellin' healthy ANARCHY. But as long as you're addicts YOU'LL BE FULL OF SHIT.

He gives them their doses. They quaff them down.

METHADONE CLINIC, EXTERIOR, DAY

Sid and Nancy push through the crowd of addicts waiting outside.

NANCY
Fuck that guy telling us what to do.

ADDICT
Hey, don't push!

SID
Don't worry about him.

ANOTHER ADDICT
Look who it ain't — Sid Vicious!

ANOTHER ADDICT
I'm SCARED!!

Somebody tousles Sid's 'do'. Pissed, Sid lashes out. He catches a fist, trips and falls. Nancy lands several good punches, protecting Sid. Sid pulls a switchblade from his boot, but somebody else grabs it from him.

SID
NANCEEEEEEE . . .

MAX'S KANSAS CITY, INTERIOR, DAY

Nancy sits opposite the manager. She has a black eye. She holds Sid's portfolio. Her old friend, Trell, has come along for moral support.

TRELL
Come on, Vito. Don't be such a jerk.

MANAGER
I'm just not sure how many people want to see Sid Vicious on his own —

NANCY
ARE YOU KIDDING? SID VICIOUS IS A MAJOR STAR.

TRELL
(Interrupting Nancy) He's not gonna be on his OWN. He's gonna have a fucking great back-up band behind him.

MANAGER
Yeah? Who?

NANCY
Who? Who? Iggy! Dee Dee! Chrissie! Debbie! It's true!
DEBBIE HARRY is gonna be singing back up. Johnny
Thunders! Joe Strummer! Stiv Bators! Jerry Nolan . . .

MANAGER
(Laughing) I love you, Nancy. You're a fucking nutcase.
But I'm running a business here. You really think he can pull
this off? CAN HE PLAY?

NANCY
He can! He can! He practises all the time! (To Trell) Right?

Trell shows signs of doubt.

NANCY
Vito, please give us a gig. You want me to fuck you?

MANAGER
No. And you shouldn't offer. It's not professional.

The manager lights a cigarette. Tense pause. The phone rings. Nancy takes
it off the hook, slams it down on the desk.

MANAGER
All right. I'll give you three grand for three gigs.

Nancy and Trell squeal with delight. Nancy holds out her hand.

NANCY
DEAL.

———— ———— ———— ———— ———— ————

CHELSEA HOTEL, ROOM 201, INTERIOR, DAY

The door is open. Sid and their neighbour, Wax Max, strum guitars in front
of the TV. Wax Max is Trell's boyfriend. Nancy pushes in with bags of
groceries and artificial logs.

NANCY
Sid! Sid! Hey, Max. Sid, guess what? Sid, I did it! I got you
three gigs at Max's. At least three. Maybe more. Aren't you
EXCITED!

SID
(Nodding) Yeah . . .

NANCY
Sid. What's going on?

107

SID

(Guilty) We're just jamming . . . you know . . .

WAX MAX

Watching 'Trigger'.

NANCY

Oh YEAH?

Her eyes scour the room. Among the garbage she spies a syringe. She snatches it up.

NANCY

SID, what's THIS? Sid?! *(Turning to Wax Max)* Did you give him this?

TRELL

Fucking come on, Nancy.

WAX MAX

I just came here to jam, all right. Just be cool.

NANCY

Don't tell me to BE COOL. Sid! SID! We had a DEAL! We said we weren't going to do any more smack till after the GIG! YOU ASSHOLE! YOU FUCKING JERK!

Nancy shoves Sid. Sid grunts. Max gets up and leaves with Trell, taking his guitar. Nancy rails at Sid.

WAX MAX

Later, y'all.

NANCY

Shit! I can't trust you as far as I can fucking THROW YOU! We had a deal! We said we weren't going to do any smack TILL AFTER THE GIG! And you haven't EVEN SAVED ME ANY, YOU FUCKHEAD. Shit, you ASSHOLE! MOTHERFUCKING JERK!

She thwacks him with a pillow. He slugs her, then gets up, kicks the door and stumbles out.

NANCY

(Following) Sid!

————— ————— ————— ————— ————— —————

CHELSEA HOTEL, STAIRCASE, INTERIOR, DAY

Out of it, Sid pauses at the top of the stairs. He takes one step, blacks out and falls, tumbling headlong to the lower landing. Trell comes running up.

TRELL

What the fuck is going on? Oh, shit! Is he all right?

NANCY

NO! HE'S A FUCKING! ASSHOLE! JUNKY!

TRELL

Don't fucking kick him! Do you think he's broken any bones or anything?

NANCY

No. He's still breathing. *(Kicks him again.)*

TRELL

Nancy, help me take him to my room. Come on.

Nancy and Trell heave Sid down the corridor. Sid is out cold. Up the stairs come the hotel manager and two prospective guests.

MANAGER

You're really gonna love this place. A lot of great artists stay here. I want you to stay a long time . . . *(He sees Sid and Nancy. Makes an abrupt turn.)* It's a couple of my ah, foreign exchange students. Why don't we just get to the elevator, OK? We'll take the elevator.

———— ———— ———— ———— ———— ————

MAX'S KANSAS CITY, EXTERIOR, NIGHT

Fire trucks hurtle past. The line extends around the block . . .

———— ———— ———— ———— ———— ————

MAX'S KANSAS CITY, INTERIOR, NIGHT

Sid bounds on stage.

SID

Do you want to hear 'My Way', arseholes?! *(positive response)* Well! I've forgotten it! Eins, zwei, eins, zwei, drei . . .

Sid and the band launch into 'Something Else'. Sid nearly falls. Wild applause. The band is really tight. Sid is awestruck and delighted. A bouncer guards a box labelled: 'Kute! Kitties! Free!' The box is surrounded by cooing girls in fearsome punk attire.

BOUNCER

Hey, Nancy! You want a kitty?

NANCY

Where?

BOUNCER
Gotta get rid of all six of 'em.

Nancy goes over, looks in the box and picks a kitten.

NANCY
I want this one! He LIKES me!!

BAR, INTERIOR, LATER

Sid, Nancy, Trell and the band sit at a table after the gig. Sweaty and exhausted, snorting lines of coke. All have kittens.

NANCY
(Clutching a kitten) You were great! You were so fuckin'
great!

SID
Yeah, well, I don't know about that. I mean most of the
people there were screaming for John and throwing drugs
and shit at me.

TRELL
That's just cause they love you, man. They're your fans.

GUITARIST
It would have gone off a lot better if we'd rehearsed.

NANCY
He doesn't NEED to rehearse. Sid's a natural.

SID
Yeah. A natural fuck up.

DRUMMER
You could get it together, Sid. If you just learn the words . . .

NANCY

Words! Only bridge and tunnel geeks worry about fucking words. Shit!

SID

Yeah. My WAY . . .

WAX MAX

Hey, Sid, don't go gittin' down on yourself, man. If we just worked a little harder. You know . . .

NANCY

Oh, what do you know?

WAX MAX

Hey, Nancy, be cool, all right! I'm just trying to help Sid out . . .

NANCY

Everybody LIKES Sid. Nobody likes the shit you do.

GUITARIST

Nancy, be cool . . .

WAX MAX

Hey, Nancy, don't worry about it. People will be into my stuff around 85, 86. All right?

NANCY

Yeah. Well you're LUCKY to be in Sid's band. You all are.

GUITARIST

Nancy, be cool . . .

NANCY

FUCK YOU! God! Shut the fuck up! EVERYTHING WAS FINE! It was going REALLY WELL! We don't fucking DESERVE this! ASSHOLE *(She storms off.)*

SID

(Addressing them all) Er – look – see you at rehearsal.

The band are speechless. Sid follows Nancy towards the exit. A group of teeny punks approach him.

PUNKETTE

Hey, Sid! We saw your show at Max's!

SID

Oh, yeah. What d'you think of it?

PUNKETTES

(In unison) YOU SUCK!!

The punkettes laugh and congratulate themselves on their more-vicious-

than-Vicious attitude. Nancy and Sid are devastated.

> NANCY
> I want them 86'd PERMANENTLY!

BIG TAXI, INTERIOR, NIGHT

Nancy and Sid. The new kitten has emerged from Nancy's leather jacket.

> NANCY
> Listen, those guys are full of shit. Listen to me, Sid. I know what's best for you. That's why I'm your MANAGER. Right?

> SID
> Yeah.

> NANCY
> 'Learn the fucking words.' You don't need to learn the fucking words. Just make 'em up like you did on 'My Way'. Huh.

> SID
> Wish we had some more coke.

> NANCY
> We can get some. Don't you worry about anything. Don't worry about drugs. Don't worry about the band. Don't worry about gigs. I'm gonna take care of EVERYTHING. That's what I'm here for. Everything's gonna be fine.

Sid, very docile, lays his head on Nancy's shoulder.

CHELSEA HOTEL, ROOM 201, INTERIOR, NIGHT

Nancy and Sid in bed. TV on. Much junk paraphernalia in evidence. Sid is comatose.

> NANCY
> Sid. Sid.

> SID
> Mmmm . . .

> NANCY
> I must have been dreaming . . . I thought we had this little dog . . . it was really little — and we loved it . . . but, then, it got sick and — it was dead . . .

> SID
> Ahhh . . .

NANCY

Yeah . . . it was dead . . . and we loved it . . . and we didn't
know where to bury it in New York . . . wanted to keep it . . .
so we ate it . . .

SID

Ahhh . . .

A loud banging on the door. Sid and Nancy react slowly.

VOICE

SID! You're supposed to be on stage! RIGHT NOW!

MAX'S KANSAS CITY, INTERIOR, NIGHT

*Sid attempts to perform 'I Wanna Be Your Dog', reading the lyrics from a
piece of paper. Showers of dollar bills and papers collide with him on stage.
John is sitting at a table. Sid freezes mid-song and sits down on the stage.
John is gone.*

CHELSEA HOTEL, ROOM 201, INTERIOR, DAY

John is being interviewed on TV. Sid runs a knife across Nancy's back. Nancy sits opening the papers he's collected.

NANCY
They're all EMPTY! . . . just little paper squares . . .

SID
Where you going?

NANCY
Get some more . . .

———— ———— ———— ———— ———— ————

ALPHABET CITY, EXTERIOR, DAY

Gretchen waits on the street corner of a shattered neighbourhood. Sid and Nancy stumble towards her. Burning braziers, subway steam, suspicious characters, panhandlers.

NANCY
Gretchen!

GRETCHEN
We have to go into that building.

They pass four or five Puerto Rican kids on the way. Beating up on the littlest one. Sid takes offence.

KIDS
Where is the money?
I want that money!

SID
Oy! Cut it out. Let 'im go.

KID
He owes us three bucks, man.

SID
I don't care. Leave 'im alone.

KID
Who the hell do you think you are?

SID
Sid Vicious.

Disbelief turns to horror. Sid's lip curls. The kids run away. Sid laughs, wraps around Nancy. The three of them walk on together.

NANCY
Good, Sid! That was good!

GRETCHEN
We have to go into that building.

———— ———— ———— ———— ———— ————

CHELSEA HOTEL, ROOM 201, INTERIOR, SUNSET

Gretchen is with them in the room, trading drugs for cash. Sid and Nancy are barely aware of her presence.

GRETCHEN
So then I went backstage and there were all these other girls there and he came up to me — he really likes me — and he asked me if I had any drugs and I said yes — they're back at my house — so we went back to my house . . . he really likes me . . . some people say he's really ugly but he's NOT — he's really cute — there's something about him that's really cool — I don't know what it is, Nance . . . He does . . . he likes me. He said he's going to England next week and he might take me — which would be so cool — just like you did — it was great! . . . this is really great dope . . . I don't know . . . likes me though — I know that. Said he was going to write a song about me . . . be a really good song . . .

———— ———— ———— ———— ———— ————

SUBWAY, INTERIOR, DAY

Nancy and Sid ride the train downtown. Nancy is pissed. Sid is hurting now. Opposite them sit two Puerto Rican kids — about 18 and 19 — wearing new leather jackets and clean jeans. The boy has slicked black hair. The girl wears lots of lipstick. They are fairly disgusted by Sid and Nancy's condition.

SID
My bones hurt . . .

116

4TH STREET AND AVENUE D, EXTERIOR, DAY

Dozens of people stand around at the back of an old seedy tenement block. Blacks, Puerto Ricans, middle-class whites. Bowery Snax is one of them. He slaps around the smallest person in line.

> BOWERY
> Where were you? . . . Fucking where? . . . Wrong, wrong.
> **WRONG!**

Nancy drags Sid out of the subway station. As they approach the group a bucket on a rope is being lowered from a top floor.

> NANCY
> Yo, Bowery!

> BOWERY
> Sid! Nancy! What's going on?

The bucket has reached eye level. A woman removes something. The line shuffles forward. Bowery immediately procures 'next-in-line' for Sid and Nancy.

> BOWERY
> Excuse me, man. This is Sid Vicious here.

They put money in the bucket. It ascends.

CHELSEA HOTEL, ROOM 201, INTERIOR, DAY

Bowery and Sid look on as Nancy shoots up. It is a big hit and she nods before the needle leaves her arm. Bowery removes the works and prepares for his hit. Nancy lays on her side on the bed.

> BOWERY
> It's none of my business, man, but I don't know why you hang with this chick. Fucking junk-hog. Let's face it. Top of that she's always getting down on you, bitchin' at you, complaining . . . Shit . . .

> SID
> She's all right. She don't mean it.

> BOWERY
> She oughta have more respect for you. If I had a girlfriend she'd show me some respect. Believe it.

> SID
> What are you talking about? Respect. You don't know her. She's got me those gigs at Max's. We're both getting off the H . . .

BOWERY
Smart move. My turn?

SID
Yeah . . . maybe . . .

BOWERY
Don't get me wrong, Sid. Nancy's great! I love her. You know what I'm saying . . . Did I leave a lot of money around here? I left a fucking lot of money someplace. I thought I might have left it here . . .

Sid, his arm round Nancy, stares blankly at Bowery.

BOWERY
Can I have a little bit of this for later? Sid? Just a little . . .

CHELSEA HOTEL, ROOM 201, INTERIOR, NIGHT

Junks on TV. Sid and Nancy sit in bed, feeding each other cold takeaway Chinese food. The kitten prowls over the bed. They eat very little.

SID
When was the last time we fucked?

NANCY
I don't remember. We can if you want to . . .

SID
Nah. Just give me a kiss.

They kiss. Their phone rings, distant and ignored.

BACK ALLEY, EXTERIOR, DAY

Sid and Nancy kiss in a back alley, oblivious to the garbage cans falling all around them.

——— ——— ——— ——— ——— ———

CHELSEA HOTEL, ROOM 201, INTERIOR, DAY/NIGHT

Sid and Nancy sit at a table. Nancy has finished shooting up, struggles to get up, stumbles into something and falls down. Crash. Sid, shooting up glances over at her. He returns to his safety pin, eye dropper and bloody hole . . .

——— ——— ——— ——— ——— ———

VIVISECTION LAB, INTERIOR, NIGHT

A lab-coated doctor sticks a long needle into a rat's brain. Sid and Nancy are prize guests at a black tie party in the lab. Huge models of neurons and the human brain. Nancy overhears a doctor talking to Sid . . .

> DOCTOR
> I said petit mal syndrome. It's what you suffer from. That's why your eye is closed and you nod out all the time.

Nancy smiles. She puts her hand into a Bunsen burner flame and holds it there.

——— ——— ——— ——— ——— ———

CHELSEA HOTEL, ROOM 201, INTERIOR, DAY

> NANCY
> OWW!

Sid's cigarette has burned Nancy. She grabs it, tosses it away. It smoulders for a long time. Sid and Nancy watch as it burns. The room fills with smoke. Curtains and clothes catch fire. They watch the place ablaze.

*Firemen kick the door down. Chemical foam sprays everywhere. Sid and
Nancy haven't moved. They are virtually carried out of the room.*

CHELSEA HOTEL, STAIRCASE, INTERIOR, DAY

*Nancy and Sid covered in flecks of foam, push past firemen and residents,
lugging their Harrods bags downstairs. They are accompanied by the manager.
Stain, the old porter, follows slowly behind them with Sid's guitar. More
firemen run upstairs.*

> MANAGER
> Do you have any idea who has stayed here before you?
> Dylan Thomas, Thomas Wolfe, Arthur Miller, Tennessee
> Williams. This is not a place where people set fire to their
> rooms. The Chelsea Hotel is a landmark . . . It's a historic
> part of the city of New York . . .

They pass a junky. The Chelsea Child runs at Stain.

> CHELSEA CHILD
> Shoppin! I want shoppin! I want shoppin! Shoppin! . . .

CHELSEA HOTEL, ROOM 100, INTERIOR, DAY

The manager, Sid and Nancy approach the new room.

> MANAGER
> I'm putting you right in here, in Room 100. It's on the first
> floor — you won't even have to wait for the elevator. You'll
> like it! . . . Wait a second! Wait a second! Excuse me. Where
> are you going with that lamp?

> NANCY
> *(Entering the room)* This is our lamp.

> MANAGER
> You can't move furniture from room to room. I . . . I forget
> where the FIXTURES are . . .

> NANCY
> It's OUR lamp. We bought it.

*The manager follows Nancy into the room. Radiator noises. Scratching
sounds. Sid is already lying down on the bed.*

> SID
> Where's the TV?

> MANAGER
> There's no TV? *(Turns to Stain who has finally made it)*

120

There's no TV! *(Turns back to Sid)* Look. Would you do me a favour? Go up to your old room — get the television set — and bring it down.

Nancy dumps her purse down on the bed. A lot of money spills out.

MANAGER
Look — Look, forget about the damages! I'll add them to your bill . . .

STAIN
He wants you to like this room. *(Drops Sid's guitar on the floor)* Bob Dylan was born here.

——— ——— ——— ——— ——— ———

FAST FOOD, TIMES SQUARE, INTERIOR, DAY

Sid and Nancy sit near the window talking to Gretchen. They all look sick and nurse big Cokes.

GRETCHEN
I haven't got anything. Just my wake-up shot. Nobody's holding downtown.

SID
Bowery said he'd meet us here.

GRETCHEN
You guys still buying off Bowery? I heard he sold someone a paper and they DIED.

SID
That's fucking bullshit! *(He gets up and stamps outside.)*

GRETCHEN
You guys still fighting, Nance?

NANCY
He's real depressed.

GRETCHEN
Yeah. Jimmy's real depressed too.

Sid starts banging on the window.

GRETCHEN
He broke three of my ribs. We're being so stupid, Nance. We
should just leave 'em.

Nancy watches Sid, standing outside, screaming at her.

NANCY
Yeah, sure. Love kills. See ya. *(She hurries after Sid.)*

———— ———— ———— ———— ———— ————

PLAYLAND, EXTERIOR, DAY

*Nancy crosses Times Square and joins Sid talking to a kid hustler. The
hustler shakes his head. Sid marches up and down.*

SID
FUCK FUCK FUCK FUCK FUCK FUCK!

*Nancy stares in the window of the fake ID store. Prominently displayed are
two matching 007 knives.*

NANCY
Look, Sid. You like those?

———— ———— ———— ———— ———— ————

CHELSEA HOTEL, ROOM 100, INTERIOR, NIGHT

*Sid turns the place over, looking for drugs. Nancy lays on her side on the
bed, moaning.*

NANCY
My kidneys hurt. Sid, where'd you put it?

SID
I CAN'T REMEMBER!

NANCY
You did it without me.

SID
Oh, come on. If I only had enough for one of us, I'd give it
all to you.

NANCY
Liar!

Sid reaches blind into a drawer and cuts his finger on a razor.

> SID
> Poxy fucking thing! Fuck it!

> NANCY
> You hate me. . .

> SID
> I don't. I DON'T.

> NANCY
> I wish I was fuckin' dead.

> SID
> Shut up! Don't keep going on about it. I got more reasons to
> be depressed than you. You're much better off than I am.

> NANCY
> Why? At least you USED to be something. I've never been
> ANYTHING.

*They hear a sound in the hall. Sid hurries to the door and opens it. He looks
out to see . . .*

——————— ——————— ——————— ——————— ——————— ———————

CHELSEA HOTEL, HALL, INTERIOR, NIGHT

*The Chelsea Child at the door across from theirs bringing in the newspaper
and a bottle of Galliano.*

CHELSEA HOTEL, ROOM 100, INTERIOR, NIGHT

Sid shuts the door.

> NANCY
> Is it Bowery?

> SID
> Nah. It's that dwarf.

> NANCY
> It's not a dwarf, Sid. It's a little boy.

> SID
> What would you know! Little kids don't dress like that!

> NANCY
> Oh, fuck you!

> SID
> Fuck you, too!!

Nancy starts to whimper.

> SID
> Look, I'm sorry . . . I'm sorry. I wish we had something to
> hit too.

> NANCY
> I wish we could get out of here . . .

> BOWERY'S VOICE
> Sid! Nance! Pull up your pants!

*The door swings open. In comes Bowery Snax. Sid and Nancy jump up,
hungry little animals scrambling for their dinner.*

> NANCY
> Bowery!

> SID
> What you got?

> BOWERY
> Not much. You got any soda or anything?

> NANCY
> Oh, come on! Don't fuck around! We got the cash.

> BOWERY
> Everybody's got the cash. But nobody's holding. I've been up
> and down this island twice today. Been all the way to
> Brooklyn. Hate that fuckin' town. *(Turns to Sid and reaches
> in his coat)* I've been reading this book —

Nancy interrupts him.

NANCY

Oh, come on! Don't fuck around you slimehole! Just give it to us!

BOWERY

I'm sorry. I can't hear you. What is it you're saying?

NANCY

I said you were a fucking slime hole.

BOWERY

Don't FUCKING talk to me — you stupid little slut —

SID

OY! OY! I don't want to hear all your CRAP. Just give us what you got, or fuck off! Jesus!

BOWERY

Right. Hey, easy, easy . . . *(Produces candy bar)* Here —

SID

Fucking toerag.

Sid tries to go for Bowery. Bowery knocks him aside.

BOWERY

Don't get up, Sid. I was just leaving.

NANCY

Wait!

BOWERY

FUCK YOU, NANCY! You people are RUDE!

NANCY

I'm sorry.

BOWERY

(Halts at the door) Excuse me. I couldn't hear.

NANCY

I'm sorry.

BOWERY

(Walking back in) You better be. You better watch your step you know. The buzz is out on you. Here! *(Throws packet on floor and sits down.)*

NANCY

What's this?

SID

(Holding up packet) What's this?

BOWERY

Speed.

NANCY
Sulphate?!

SID
You want some of this? You want this?

NANCY
Yeah.

SID
Yeah.

BOWERY
I never touch that stuff, man. It makes me paranoid. You guys are outside, man. If you shoot that stuff, it's gonna make you sick.

NANCY
What about the Dilaudid?

BOWERY
I tried. Couldn't get a hold of the guy. You got a phone? I'll try again.

NANCY
It's in the lobby.

BOWERY
The phone is in the lobby! Right! No promises. But — for my famous friends — I'll go the extra mile. You guys aren't going anywhere, are you? *(He exits).*

━━━━ ━━━━ ━━━━ ━━━━ ━━━━ ━━━━

CHELSEA HOTEL, ROOM 100, INTERIOR, LATER

Sid sits in a chair strumming bass. Nancy stares at the TV.

NANCY
My eyes hurt. The TV's so bright it hurts my eyes.

No response from Sid. A fuse blows and the amp and room lights die. The bathroom lights remain.

SID
Oh, fuck it.

━━━━ ━━━━ ━━━━ ━━━━ ━━━━ ━━━━

CHELSEA HOTEL, ROOM 100, INTERIOR, LATER

Sid and Nancy sit in a corner of the room.

SID
This bloke — German bloke — he was killed in a crash — and he uh — lost his head — it was cut off . . . his head . . . and

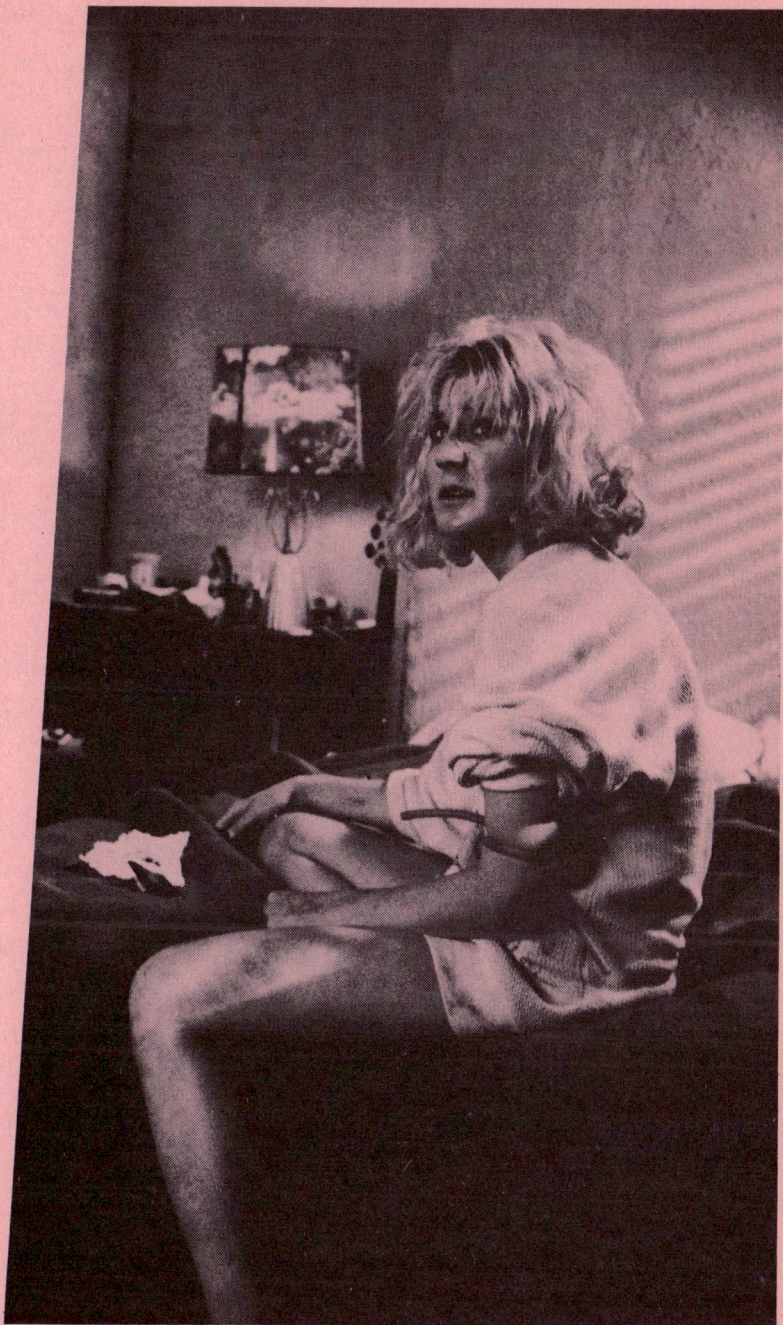

these men — scientists — they saved this head and — um —
they like talked to it — it could communicate to them . . .
it like blinked — you know — um — blinked to them . . .
they'd know what it was saying . . .

> NANCY
> Shut up, listen to me.

———— ———— ———— ———— ———— ————

CHELSEA HOTEL, ROOM 100, INTERIOR, LATER

Sid is standing at the window. Nancy is on the bed.

> SID
> I don't want to. . .

> NANCY
> Why not?

> SID
> I don't know. I just don't.

> NANCY
> What're you waiting for? Bowery?

> SID
> Bowery doesn't fucking matter.

> NANCY
> *(Toying with a knife)*
> What does?

———— ———— ———— ———— ———— ————

YANKEE LIQUORS, INTERIOR, NIGHT

*Sid and Nancy drift in. They head for the refrigerator. They select champagne.
They are very wired and weird . . .*

> SID
> Why don't we just OD?

> NANCY
> That's not GLORIOUS. We gotta go at the same time. Like
> that movie of the week where those kids — they ran their car
> into a train.

> SID
> We don't have a car.

> NANCY
> That doesn't matter. It's not important. The important thing
> is that we go together. That's the thing.

They approach the counter. Nancy tests a bottle against her cheek.

> NANCY
> These aren't cold! Champagne is supposed to be cold.

> SALESMAN
> They're cold. They're cold.

> NANCY
> Are you sure?

> SALESMAN
> Trust me!

Sid stares at his reflection in the case. The salesman rings the bottles up.

> What, are you having a party?

> SID
> Yeah.

> NANCY
> Fuck you! Fuck you and your stupid questions. Just for that we're never coming back! Sid! Sid!

Nancy grabs Sid's arm and leads him out of the door.

──── ──── ──── ──── ──── ────

WAX MAX'S ROOM, INTERIOR, NIGHT

Trell opens the door. Sid and Nancy stand there, very strange. Max is watching Ugly George.

> TRELL
> Hi guys! What's going on?

> NANCY
> Will you hold this stuff for us?

They have armloads of their belongings—Sid's gold records, his portfolio, a bundle of letters, miscellaneous stuff.

> TRELL
> Sure.

> WAX MAX
> What's up?

> NANCY
> We don't want to get ripped off.

> WAX MAX
> I hear that.

Nancy looks at Sid. Sid stares into space then moves into the room.

TRELL
(To Nancy) **Are you all right?**

SID
Have you got a joint?

MAX
Not really, man.

NANCY
Sid. The jacket.

Sid nods, remembering. He drops his leather jacket on to the bed, turns and stares at Nancy then follows her out of the room. Mewing, Nancy's kitten comes creeping out of the pocket.

————— ————— ————— ————— ————— —————

CHELSEA HOTEL, ROOM 100, INTERIOR, NIGHT

Sid is sitting on the bed, smoking a cigarette.

SID
I'm just not going to. OK.

NANCY
You have to. You promised.

SID
Yeah, well, I changed me mind.

NANCY
You can't change your mind! We said we'd go together. You can't change your mind!

SID
'Course I can. I just did. I did!

NANCY
NO! Blaze of glory! You promised! You promised! *(Hits him.)*

SID
No! I'm getting out of this poxy place. I'm going back to England —

NANCY
NO! Why?

SID
'Cos I want to get straight. I wanna be with my friends. People who care. . .

NANCY
OK! OK! Just leave me!

SID

You're always putting fuckin' words in my mouth. DID I SAY THAT I WOULD FUCKING LEAVE YOU—NO I FUCKING DID NOT!!

NANCY

I'm your best friend, Sid . . .

SID

So you keep fucking telling me.

NANCY

. . . and you'll never get straight. You say that EVERY FUCKING DAY. It's the SAME. I can't get up tomorrow to the same thing. I can't do it anymore. Oh, God, please help me. Please, you PROMISED.

SID

You're so full of shit, you know. You're so fucking blind.

NANCY

NO, I'm not. I'm not blind. I see everything. Where are you going?

SID

I'm going up the off-licence.

NANCY

(Tries to bar the door) It's five o'clock in the morning! There's nothing out there.

Nancy hangs on to him. They struggle.

SID

Get out of the fucking way!

NANCY

Help me! Fuck you, Sid. You're so stupid!

SID
FUCK OFF OUT THE FUCKING WAY!

NANCY
You're so fucking weak and stupid! HELP ME!
(Hits him again.)

Sid falls on to the bed and grabs a knife.

SID
YOU WANT TO DIE?! YOU WANT TO FUCKIN' DIE?

NANCY
YES!

She lunges forward. The knife cuts her. Nancy gets really mad. They fight more, falling tangled to the floor, breathing heavily. Sid coughs. Nancy sobs and cries.

I hate this. Oh, God I hate this.

SID
I feel really sick . . .

———— ———— ———— ———— ———— ————

CHELSEA HOTEL, ROOM 100, INTERIOR, LATER

Nancy and Sid lie in bed making up.

NANCY
There were these guys in this band . . . one time . . . they go . . . Let's throw someone out the window . . . Let's throw Nancy. They wanted to set me on fire and throw me out. I said go ahead. Sounds like a great way of dying . . .

SID
What happened?

NANCY
They chickened out.

SID
(Falling asleep) **Just like Simon . . .** *(He snores.)*

———— ———— ———— ———— ———— ————

CHELSEA HOTEL, ROOM 100, INTERIOR, LATER

Nancy struggles out of bed. She advances slowly and painfully towards the bathroom. Sees her bloody torso in the mirror.

NANCY
Sid . . . *(Falls down hard.)* **Sid . . .**

Sid is fast asleep.

CHELSEA HOTEL, ROOM 100, INTERIOR, EARLY MORNING

Light creeps through the slatted shutters. Sid sits on the bloodstained bed gazing at Popeye on TV. Catatonic he plays with the knife.

Bowery Snax returns. He calls from outside the door.

> BOWERY'S VOICE
> You guys awake? There's something here for you! Want to check it out?

The door opens to the extent of the safety chain.

Bowery appears. He sees Nancy lying on the bathroom floor.

> BOWERY
> Oh, Sid. This is a serious fuck-up, man. *(Turns to leave)* Bad scene!

Sid is still holding the knife, staring at the TV.

23RD STREET, EXTERIOR, MORNING

Bowery heads east for the subway. He passes a pair of pay phones. Backtracks, dials three digits hastily.

> BOWERY
> *(Affecting an English accent)* 'Allo guv'nor. Someone's bin 'urt. Chelsea 'Otel. Room 100. That's right. Can't stop. Cheerio.

———— ———— ———— ———— ———— ————

CHELSEA HOTEL, ROOM 100, INTERIOR, DAY

Very tight on Sid as he sits on the bloodstained bed. His face is a blank.

> DETECTIVE'S VOICE
> Who called 911?

No response.

CHELSEA HOTEL, LOBBY, INTERIOR, DAY

As Sid is escorted through the lobby, the reporters move in and flashbulbs start to pop.

> REPORTERS
> **There he is! That's Sid Vicious! That's Sid Vicious!**

Sid's demeanour shifts.

> SID
> **I'LL SMASH YOUR FUCKING CAMERAS!**

The detectives shove Sid through the lobby doors.

——————— ——————— ——————— ——————— ——————— ———————

RIKER'S ISLAND, INTERIOR, DAY

Sid sits on the floor. Hunched up foetally. Cold turkey. No belt, no shoes, no socks. He keeps switching positions. Every position is intolerable.

Another junky occupies the single bench, shaking.

The door opens.

> GUARD'S VOICE
> You're out of here, punk. Somebody paid the fifty grand.

——————— ——————— ——————— ——————— ——————— ———————

F. LEE BAILEY'S OFFICE, INTERIOR, DAY

Sid sits with Malcolm, his mum and the great lawyer. They're on the 28th floor of the Empire State Building.

> MALCOLM
> **This is Mr. F. Lee Bailey, Sid. He's a famous barrister. He's agreed to take your case.**

> BAILEY
> Pleased to meet you . . . Sid.

> SID
> What do I need a lawyer for?

> MUM
> Because you're not guilty, Simon. You're not guilty.

> SID
> How do you know?

Bailey coughs uncomfortably, looks away.

> BAILEY
> Damned pigeons.

MALCOLM
Let's have none of that now, Sidney. Paul and Steve are coming out here. For the REUNION. You're about to be a busy boy.

SID
(Crying, mumbling) Fuck it.

BAILEY
Pardon me.

SID
All I want is Nancy.

MALCOLM
Don't be so fucking silly, Sid. Nancy's gone. You're still around. You've got to start behaving sensibly.

MUM
He's a bit upset right now, Mr Bailey. He doesn't know what he wants. You tell him what to say. He's a good boy.

Wings flutter outside. Sid looks away.

———— ———— ———— ———— ———— ————

MAX'S KANSAS CITY, EXTERIOR, NIGHT

A line around the block. Graffiti on the walls read, Sid Vicious is innocent, Nancy RIP. Lots of noise.

———— ———— ———— ———— ———— ————

MAX'S KANSAS CITY, INTERIOR, NIGHT

Sid drinks alone at the bar. Someone comes and sits down beside him. Wally from long ago. Wally is older and blonder. Speaks with a Midatlantic drawl.

WALLY
Sid! All right, mate?

SID
Oh, yeah. How's it going?

WALLY
All right. Yeah . . . Shit, Sid. I'm real sorry about Nancy . . . Everybody . . . I was in London . . . you know. . .

SID
So what you up to?

WALLY
Living out here now. Got a band. Guess who I saw the other day? Do you remember Olive? That really DRASTIC bird. Yeah. She's off smack now. She's like all pink and really pretty. Got a little kid. Do you want another drink?

                    SID
              (Nods) **Yeah.**

Wally heads off. Hugh Kares walks in and sits down next to Sid.

                    HUGH
              **SO, SIDNEY! Long time no see! Hey, I'm really broken up
              about the news, I mean, my condolences. Really, man, I'm
              sorry.**

Sid looks away. Wally returns with a beer bottle.

                    HUGH
              So, Sidney, who's handling you now?

*Sid grabs the bottle and lashes out with it. Beer splashes all over Hugh. The
bottle hits Wally in the face. Hugh flees. Sid rises, stares at Wally writhing on
the floor.*

Bouncers jump Sid. Sirens sound.

                    SID
              FUCKING HELL!

—— —— — —— ——

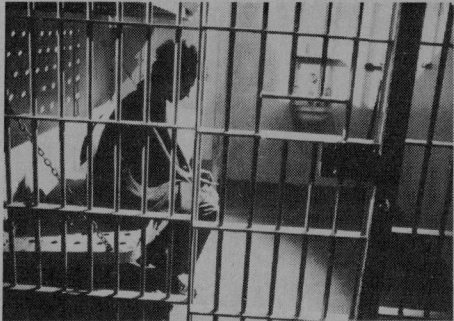

JAIL CELL, INTERIOR, NIGHT

*Sid stares at the naked lightbulb. Reaches up and unscrews it. Darkness. The
bulb smashes on the floor. Sid saws at his wrists. Blood spatters.*

—— —— —— —— —— ——

JAIL HOUSE, INTERIOR, DAY

*Sid stands at a counter, getting his possessions back. His wrists are thickly
bandaged. He faces two cops — one, keen and young, the other, old and wise.*

                    YOUNG COP
              (Planting things on the counter) **One candy bar, one piece of**

string, one piece of paper, one pack of cigarettes . . .

OLD COP
You know, you're out on bail again, kid.

YOUNG COP
Six books of matches . . .

OLD COP
Why don't you give yourself a break?

YOUNG COP
One subway token . . .

OLD COP
I know you think you're kind of tough . . . *(Searching for Sid's name on the roster.)* Richie.

YOUNG COP
One safety pin . . .

OLD COP
But there's a lot of guys —

YOUNG COP
One stick of gum . . .

OLD COP
— tougher than you that wish they was wearing your shoes right now.

YOUNG COP
One leather-studded armband . . .

OLD COP
You know, you can walk out that door and you can stay out for good —

YOUNG COP
Sixty-seven cents . . .

OLD COP
Or you can turn right around and walk back in here again.

YOUNG COP
(Takes a breath) And $540 cash. Sign here please.

Sid signs and stuffs his pockets. He hasn't heard a word.

OLD COP
You know, it's all up to you, Richie. I don't see any braces on your legs.

Sid nods and starts to limp away as if he had braces on his legs.

                    SID
              One thing . . .

                    OLD COP
              Sure. What is it, kid?

                    SID
              Where can I get a pizza?

_____   _____   _____   _____   _____   _____

DOCKS, EXTERIOR, DAY

Grey, dark, cold day. Sid gets off the boat from Riker's Island. The first thing he sees is a pizza place.

_____   _____   _____   _____   _____   _____

PIZZA PLACE, INTERIOR, DAY

Sid sits in the window, finishing an entire pan. Steam pours from the subway vents outside. Three kids watch him through the glass. Sid wipes his mouth, kicks the table over and leaves.

_____   _____   _____   _____   _____   _____

DOCKS, EXTERIOR, DAY

Sid steps into the strange twilight. The three kids approach him. They have a ghetto blaster.

                    KID 1
              Yo, Sid! You want to dance with us?

                    SID
              Nah. I'm not dancing with no little kids.

                    KID 2
              Stop being so stuck up.

Sid looks up and down the road. It is deserted. Self-consciously, he taps a few steps with the kids. A checker cab appears.

Nancy is sitting in the back. She looks very pretty. Healthy, hair is glowing platinum, no track marks on her arms.

She smiles at Sid. Sid gets into the cab.

The door closes. Sid and Nancy fall into each other's arms. Through the back window we see them kiss as the taxi rolls away.

                    KID
              Boo! Kissing! Yuck!

The kids start to chase the cab, then stop and watch it disappear.

SID VICIOUS DIED OF A HEROIN
OVERDOSE ON 2ND FEBRUARY 1979

NANCY & SID R.I.P.

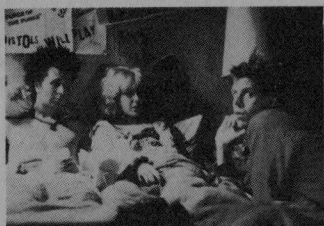

EMBASSY HOME ENTERTAINMENT
presents

SID AND NANCY

A ZENITH PRODUCTION
in association with
INITIAL PICTURES

A film by ALEX COX

—— —— —— —— ——

Sid Vicious
GARY OLDMAN

Nancy Spungen
CHLOE WEBB

—— —— —— —— ——

Director of Photography
ROGER DEAKINS

Editor
DAVID MARTIN

Music
PRAY FOR RAIN *and* THE POGUES

Co-Producer
PETER McCARTHY

Written by
ALEX COX & ABBE WOOL

Producer
ERIC FELLNER

Director
ALEX COX

Distributed in the UK by Palace Pictures

Punks + Safety Pins
- easily identifiable & challengable social stains
→ Safety into sadism, raffles into Nightmare

LOVE KILLS